THEY ME

Simon Cheshire has written stories since he was at school, but it was only after turning thirty that he realized "my mental age would never exceed ten and that, in children's books, I had finally found my natural habitat". He is the author of *Totally Unsuitable for Children* and three funny stories about schoolboy secret agent Jeremy Brown – *Jeremy Brown of the Secret Service*, *Jeremy Brown and the Mummy's Curse* and *Jeremy Brown on Mars*. The stories, he claims, "are based entirely upon actual events. Only names, characters, plots, dialogue and descriptive content have been changed, to make them more believable."

Books by the same author

Jeremy Brown of the Secret Service
Jeremy Brown and the Mummy's Curse
Jeremy Brown on Mars
Totally Unsuitable for Children

THEY
MELTED HIS
BRAIN!

SIMON CHESHIRE

WALKER BOOKS
AND SUBSIDIARIES
LONDON • BOSTON • SYDNEY

To Isobel with love

First published 1999 by Walker Books Ltd
87 Vauxhall Walk, London SE11 5HJ

This edition published 2000

2 4 6 8 10 9 7 5 3 1

Text © 1999 Simon Cheshire
Cover illustration © 1999 Hunt Emerson

This book has been typeset in Sabon.

Printed in Great Britain by Cox & Wyman Ltd,
Reading, Berkshire

British Library Cataloguing in Publication Data
A catalogue record for this book is
available from the British Library.

ISBN 0-7445-7293-2

CONTENTS

EPISODE ONE

The fate of the entire world hung in the balance. Things looked hopeless.

"Nothing's hopeless," said Dirk, Hero and Saviour of the Planet. "Let's give these tentacled horrors from the stars a taste of their own medicine!"

"You mean," gasped Penelope, Heroine and Glamorous Assistant, "we reroute the energy bypass flow through the neutron accelerator, thereby causing explosive feedback into their intergalactic transport pod?"

"You bet," said Dirk. "Let's kick their teeth in!"

"Cut! Stop! No!" cried Matthew Bland, Director, Maker of Movies and Schoolboy. "Lloyd, for goodness' sake, you're a nuclear scientist. You're an intellectual. You are not going to kick anybody's teeth in!"

"I think my character would say that," said Dirk, or rather Lloyd Martin, Actor and Friend of Matthew. He scratched his thick mop of dark hair, pulled his glasses out of his top pocket and put them back on. He could now see past the tip of his nose.

"No," said Matthew, "I think your character would say what's in my carefully written and lovingly prepared script, thanks very much." He switched off the video camera and started scribbling in his ring binder marked "Production Notes".

"It really doesn't matter either way," said Penelope, or rather Julie Custard, Actress and Other Friend of Matthew. "These are dribbly monsters from the depths of space. They haven't got teeth to start with."

"Can I smack their faces in?" said Lloyd.

"No, you can't," grumbled Matthew. His stomach grumbled too. "Let's get this scene in the can, and go home. I want my tea."

Lloyd had a different idea about what Matthew wanted, but said nothing. He took up his position, crouching in the bushes. His glasses were whipped off and popped back into his pocket. He could now no longer see past the tip of his nose. Matthew switched on the camera, and checked the focus and exposure.

Lloyd tried to look heroic, peering warily around leaves in case he was spotted by

8

something with a laser gun. Julie scrambled up through the undergrowth behind him.

"Take two! Action!"

"It's hopeless, Dirk," said Julie. "The entire research station is in the slimy grip of those fiends!"

"Nothing's hopeless," said Lloyd. "Let's give these tentacled horrors from the stars a taste of their own medicine!"

"You mean," gasped Julie, "we reroute the energy bypass flow through the neutron accelerator, thereby causing explosive feedback into their intergalactic transport pod?"

"You bet," said Lloyd. "Let's go save this crazy old world of ours!"

"Cut!" shouted Matthew. "Brilliant! Fabulous!"

Camera, tripod, lights, scripts and homemade neutron accelerator were all packed away into a huge, battered canvas bag, which Matthew got Lloyd to carry: "You're the one with the longest arms." Lloyd didn't see why it shouldn't be the one with the fattest stomach who carried the bag, but said nothing.

"We could be stuck here for ever," mumbled Matthew as they waited for a gap in the flow of cars. Lloyd wiped his glasses with his thumb. They all wondered if perhaps they should have found a better location than the middle of the huge roundabout next to the Homefit DIY Superstore.

They waited patiently on that roundabout, on that Saturday afternoon. One of them was short and round, one of them was tall and walked with a slight stoop and one of them was as completely medium-sized as it's possible to be. At that moment, crossing the road seemed like a really complicated and challenging problem. However, it would soon be the least of their worries. They would have run home and hidden under their beds if they'd had the slightest idea what was going to happen to them.

Matthew's house stood at the end of a long terrace of late-Victorian dwellings. It looked out onto a wide street, with sycamore trees sprouting at regular intervals from the pavements. It certainly wasn't the sort of place that might be, for example, the focus for an alien invasion, or a hideout for double agents on the run from international assassins. This irritated Matthew quite a lot.

Once Lloyd had deposited the equipment bag by Matthew's front door, and sloped off home muttering about somewhere else he'd like to deposit it, Matthew dragged it into the hall. There it stayed, lurking by the radiator, waiting patiently for Mum to trip over it some time later.

C-RUMP!

"Matthew Bland! Move this junk!" she yelled up the stairs, with a bottle of mascara in one hand and her bruised toes in the the other.

"I'm busy editing," called Matthew from his room.

"You're busy moving this junk! Timothy will be home in a minute!"

Cut to: face of M. Bland! thought Matthew. *Anger! Terror! Loathing! Checks fiendish plan. Cut back to hall: key unlocks front door. Ka-boom. Timothy turns into little black crisp. M. Bland cackles horribly as he is carted off in police van.*

Timothy was indeed home in precisely a minute. He was sixteen, and had inherited a more impressive set of genes than his younger brother. He was smart, he had beautifully white teeth, and twenty-four minutes earlier he'd scored the winning goal in the semi-final of the Inter-Schools Challenge Cup.

"Don't worry, Mother, I'll get the bag shifted," he said, hanging his blazer up on a peg, and flicking a speck of fluff off the shoulder.

"You hear that?" yelled Mum up the stairs. "I've got one son who's good to his mother!" She turned to Timothy, who produced from behind his back a small but perfectly wrapped bunch of flowers for her. "Oh, Timothy," she cooed, adoringly. "Are you in for tea?"

He was. The three of them sat around the kitchen table. The flowers took pride of place in a vase next to the ketchup. Timothy had made the vase in his pottery class.

"I think my hay fever's coming on," grumbled Matthew, giving the vase a hard stare.

"Timothy, I nearly forgot," said Mum suddenly, holding up her hands in alarm. Her face shone in the light from the lamp that Timothy had made in his metalwork class. "There's another letter for you from the college."

"I keep telling them I don't want a teaching job, Mother. I'm doing my A-levels. Anyway, I'll be busy with rehearsals for the school concert this evening. Then I'm taking Chloe and Alison for a pizza. I should be back around 9:45, but I'll ring if I'm going to be late."

"They're lovely girls," smiled Mum, her eyelashes fluttering proudly. "There you are, Matthew, you ought to find yourself a nice girlfriend –"

"Muuuuum!"

"– instead of wasting your time making silly films."

Cut to: fifteen years in the future. M. Bland wins third BAFTA Award for Extreme Talent. Mum interviewed watching live coverage of ceremony. "I was wrong. He was right. If only I'd listened to him." Bursts into bitter tears of regret.

"Why can't you be interested in numbers?

12

The world will always need accountants."

"Muuuuum!"

"It's unhealthy. There's Martin Lloyd –"

"Lloyd Martin."

"– thin as a rake, never eats. I know he can't help the way he looks, but at least you'd think his mother would keep him indoors more. And there's you, slowly inflating! I don't know how you manage to put on so much weight. Finish your pudding."

The following Monday lunchtime, Matthew pinned home-made posters to notice boards around the school, announcing:

The WORLD PREMIERE of

THEY CAME FROM SPACE

starring Lloyd Martin, Julie Laburnam
and Matthew Bland
written, directed, produced, edited
and equipment provided by
Matthew Bland
special effects by 21st Century Bland
own the Video today – see Bland 7C

Each poster had been printed with the aid of Timothy's computer, which he'd won as first prize in a national art competition. The posters included a small wriggly graphic representing the chilling mystery of them from space.

Matthew pinned the last one to the notice

board outside the Staff Room. Then he realized he'd forgotten to mention the venue for the premiere, went round the school changing the posters with a Biro, returned to the Staff Room, changed the last one, and stood back to admire it. It was next to the hockey team fixture list and an old dog-eared diagram of the nearest fire exits. Matthew felt a strange wave of emotion welling up in his chest. This was probably pride at his artistic achievement, but possibly indigestion.

The door of the Staff Room sneaked open, letting out a low murmur of voices, and a thick fog of aftershave and despair. Mr Prunely, from the Geography department, emerged picking at his fingernails. His brown jacket had leather patches on the elbows, and his tie displayed an impressive range of food stains.

"Hallo there, Mr Bland," he said with a cheery nod. Mr Prunely was the sort of well-spoken teacher who would always address Matthew as "Mr" and other teachers by their first names. He pointed to Matthew's notice. "Ah, your latest cinematic spectacular is ready to entertain us?"

"Yes, sir, well done."

"*They Came From Space*. Sounds jolly dramatic. Science fiction?"

"Nothing gets past you, sir, does it?" said Matthew.

"Room 12, Modern Languages Block,

Thursday donkey break."

"That's dinner break, sir. My handwriting."

"Ah. I shall look forward to it, especially the latest performance from the rather talented Miss Custard. She's still adopting a stage name, I see."

"That's movie stars for you, sir."

Mr Prunely chuckled amiably, and sauntered off down the corridor. He was still chuckling amiably as he sauntered up the corridor of the Modern Languages Block on Thursday donkey break. He chuckled amiably about many things.

Mr Nailshott, Head of Modern Languages, had wheeled the department's TV and video into Room 12. His moustache looked like the business end of a toothbrush. It bristled, livelier than a military base on red alert. He was only staying to attend the premiere because he didn't trust these little swine. They'd have his beloved equipment down to a second-hand shop if he so much as left the room for a wee, he was sure of it. He would have insisted that Bland use his own machines, but the rule about not bringing valuables to school was very strict. He knew it was. He'd written it himself.

Matthew's shaking hands fluttered over the controls of the video. Everything switched on, all set. *And the Golden Lens Cap for Best Picture Made by a Young Genius on a Budget of*

£9.49, *goes to*... His heart was chattering, and his teeth were pounding. He seemed to have lost all control over what his heart and teeth were up to.

"OK, Matt?" said Lloyd.

"Yeah, I feel much better than usual. Got a good feeling about this one."

The room was rapidly filling with pupils, mostly from Matthew's year, but with a generous helping of older and younger kids. There were more than had come to see *Volcano Town*, and many more than had attended *Kevin Johnson: Midfield Surgeon*.

"My fame is spreading," said Matthew.

Lloyd gave him a quick thumbs-up sign and went to the back of the room to sit next to Julie. He had his best pen tucked away in his blazer pocket, in case he was asked for an autograph. Nobody had ever asked him for one, but he had his pen with him anyway.

Mr Prunely wandered in and sat at one of the desks. Mr Nailshott marched over to him, and whispered sharply, "Watch these little swine. I need a wee."

He was back in time to witness the moment when the blinds were shut, the lights went out, and Matthew pressed the PLAY button. Thirty-five pupils cheered, six booed and two made rude noises.

"Shut it," growled Mr Nailshott.

The opening titles started, accompanied by

16

the *dan-dan-daaaah* music Matthew had also used for one of his early works, *Giant Bacteria Ate My Brother*. The names of the cast appeared on screen.

From near the back there was a cry of "That's Custard of 7B!" followed by a swift smack around the ear from Custard of 7B. The title appeared in sizzling red letters *(shapes cut out of card and filmed in front of Mum's flame-effect gas fire)*. It was then that the giggling really got underway.

They sniggered as the aliens' spacecraft descended to Earth *(highly detailed model Matthew had spent hours on, slid along cotton threads)*. They cackled as Dirk fought the mutant spider the aliens had hidden in his fridge *(black wool wound around a wire frame, fired out of a tub of coleslaw with the aid of an elastic band)*. By the time Dirk and Penelope had found the horribly scarred body of Doug, the hapless tramp *(Matthew with ketchup and rice crispies on his face)*, the dialogue was almost inaudible beneath the howling. Two juniors had run out clutching the front of their trousers.

Matthew, crouched beside the TV, tried not to listen. He kept his eyes on the screen, watching his creation.

Stirring music on soundtrack swells into a whirlwind of emotion! Dirk is a pillar of strength against the shivering cowardice of the undergrowth! Heroically, he delivers a fearless call to action for the whole human race! "Nothing's hopeless."

"Except this load of old tosh!" quipped an anonymous wit from the audience.

"That's the roundabout by Homefit!"

"Is that Martin Lloyd? You can't tell without his glasses on!"

The twenty-five minutes of *They Came From Space* reached their explosive climax *(miniature building set alight by Lloyd's dad)* surrounded by hoots, cheers and cackles. The lights went on, the video went off. Pupils shuffled back to their classrooms, wiping tears from their eyes.

As reactions to Matthew's films usually went, this one had been pretty positive. Lloyd and Julie emerged from the desks they'd hidden under. Mr Prunely shook Matthew's hand warmly, while Mr Nailshott checked over his beloved equipment.

"Splendid!" said Mr Prunely. "Lots of imagination and technical know-how on display there, Mr Bland. Jolly well done! And well done to you too, Miss Custard, Mr Lloyd. Super acting."

"Thank you, sir," said Lloyd and Julie weakly. They went back to their classrooms, where they would enjoy a few minutes of superstar status amid cheers and raspberries.

Mr Nailshott finished winding the TV cable

around its storage hooks. "Pity you're not like your brother, Bland," he barked. "Why a rather talented young actress like Custard there gets involved in your ridiculous drivel is beyond me."

"My adoring public seems to have trouble understanding the complex genius of my cinematic vision," said Matthew through gritted teeth.

"They certainly enjoyed themselves," said Mr Prunely. "I'm sure that's a really encouraging sign."

"I care not for encouraging signs, sir," said Matthew, confidently. "I shall be sending *They Came From Space* to a number of movie production companies, along with a selection of highlights from my recent work. The artistic savages in this school will be completely gobsmacked when I start getting offers to direct major motion pictures."

EPISODE TWO

Dear Mr Blend,

Thank you for sending us your showreel of work. This has been viewed with great interest and amazement by our Creative Director, Reg Benbow-Crisp.

Unfortunately, nothing on your tape gives us any confidence that you are suited to a career in film production. But all is not lost – your tape will provide many hours of amusement at our next office party.

Yours sincerely,
Mary Ann Bright
Secretary to the Creative Director

*   *   *

Dear Mr Blond,

Thank you for sending us your videotape of sample work. This has received close attention from our Production Manager, Fred Wallaby.

Mr Wallaby has asked me to assure you that

you need never worry about whether or not you'll make it in the world of film-making. You won't. Mr Wallaby states that he has never seen such a load of old tosh in all his life, and has flung it out of the window of his office in case it contaminates any real work, done by professionals.

Yours sincerely,
Jubilee Lyne
Secretary to the Production Manager

*   *   *

Dear Mr Blind,
Thank you for submitting your tape to me. I've always been told that if you can't say anything nice, don't say anything at all. So I won't say anything at all about your scripting, your editing, your technical ability or indeed your photographic style, which only the "video diary" type of documentary film-maker would find appealing.

Yours sincerely,
Hugh Andeye
Managing Director
P.S. However, your actress is rather talented.

*   *   *

The other twelve letters had said similar things. Matthew read the last one again. Documentaries? *Documentaries?*

"Must be mad," he mumbled to himself.

He put the letters into a ring binder labelled

21

"Get Lost File". He pushed the ring binder into the tight cram of stuff under his bed, next to the very dusty cuddly rabbit which had been there, nose down, ever since the day his Auntie Pam had given it to him six years earlier.

He made a mental note to have a clear-out under that bed one of these days, but making mental notes was a pointless thing to do. If all the mental notes he'd made about having a clear-out under the bed (or tidying on top of the wardrobe, or sorting out the pile of grubby T-shirts by his desk) had actually been written down, he'd have had enough paper to line the entire house, and still have enough left over to seal next door's cat in four metre thick papier mâché.

His room was a tip. Even dirt felt unclean in there. Germs would throw themselves on bottles of bleach rather than end up in Matthew Bland's room.

It might have been easier to move around if the place hadn't been crammed with second-hand camera accessories, video recorders and tellies, plus the digital editing gear he'd bought with 30,000 years' worth of pocket money. The miles of spaghetti-like cable which linked them all together made a dangerous assault course for unwary feet. He had inherited his video camera, the start of his whole techno-mountain, after his dad had run off to join the circus during a family outing to Weston-super-Mare.

Matthew liked to think that his room was simply too small to contain his creative brilliance. Few people ever contradicted this idea, mostly because they were afraid to go in there in the first place.

It was 11:36 pm on Friday night when he squashed his Get Lost File into the stuff under the bed. Pushing in the file popped a 500-piece jigsaw out the other side, but he had more important things to think about.

He quickly set video disc machine no. 3 to record what promised to be a fascinating programme on East European cinema of the 1930s. Why they were putting on something so interesting at a quarter past three in the morning was beyond him. He made a mental note to say something withering about it in his first major TV interview.

M. Bland introduced by host, audience cheers! Standing ovation eventually subsides. M. Bland tells hilarious anecdotes about recording programmes at a quarter past three in the morning.

With the machine set, he flipped off the light, jumped into bed and pretended to be asleep, before Mum had a chance to sneak upstairs and shout "Go to sleep, young man, I don't care if it's the weekend!"

The door flew open. "Go to sleep, young man, I don't...! Oh. Night night."

* * *

"Geffl ommur tum phlei crum, fssst!"

"What?" said Julie. She smacked the phone's earpiece against her hand a couple of times to make sure her little sister hadn't poured pineapple juice into it again. "Is that you, Matt? Let me guess, you've been captured and gagged by a ruthless gang of double agents on the run from international assassins, like you always wanted? Or have you just forgotten how to talk properly?"

She heard a gulping noise. "I said, get over to my house, fast! It's incredible!" cried Matthew.

"What's incredible?"

Matthew put the phone down. Two minutes later:

"I can't, Matt," said Lloyd. "I'm doing the Geography homework you stopped me doing last weekend because we were on a round-about."

"Just get here! It's incredible!" cried Matthew.

"What's incredible?"

Matthew put the phone down.

A short while later, Julie had finished her daily tantrum in front of her parents about having her surname surgically removed. Meanwhile, Lloyd had received six more calls from Matthew. The final one ended in a threat to have his secret love for Dawn Gardner of 9C revealed to the whole school if he didn't do as he was told. With all that out of the way, the three of them gathered in Matthew's room. Julie had brought a large hanky to sit on, to avoid possible contamination.

Mum popped her head around the door. "Now, Martin Lloyd, are you absolutely sure you don't want anything to eat?"

"Lloyd Martin," said Matthew. At least, that's what he would have said if his mouth hadn't been full. What he actually said was a sudden spray of milk.

Mum was about to call him a disgusting little pig when her attention was distracted by the sound of Timothy downstairs in the hall. He was on his way out to play in the finals of the regional chess tournament (followed by lunch with his form tutor, then shopping for a new suit, returning home by mid-afternoon to mow the back lawn). Mum waved him off with a single tear of joy glistening on her cheek.

Back upstairs, Matthew's cheeks were stuffed with Wheetie Puffs. He scooped up another spoonful of them and jammed them in before he'd even got a taste of the last lot. He'd now run out of milk and was eating them dry.

"It's incredible!" he gasped.

"I wouldn't argue with that," said Julie with disgust.

Without putting down his cereal bowl, Matthew pulled a new jumbo economy-sized packet from the box by his feet. He ripped off the top and poured himself another helping. Lloyd counted six empty jumbo economy-sized packets on the windowsill.

"Is that it?" said Julie. "Your breakfast cereal is incredible?"

"You're joking!" cried Matthew, between mouthfuls. "It's full of sugar, it tastes like cotton wool! You're better off eating the box it comes in!"

"True, Wheetie Puffs are perfectly disgusting," agreed Julie.

"I'm failing Geography because of this," mumbled Lloyd, finding another empty jumbo economy-sized packet on the bookshelf.

"I've always hated them more than Timothy himself!" continued Matthew. "Until first thing this morning! Now I love them! Can't get enough of them! They're Wheetie sweetie to eat-y! They're flummph flum poolsit glorblus!"

He'd finished the bowl, and was already searching around for some more. Julie looked at Lloyd, Lloyd looked at Julie.

"And the point of dragging us over here is…?" said Julie.

Matthew waggled a video disc at them. "It's all recorded on here. Something transmitted at a quarter past three this morning. It's incredible, and I want you to see it."

"You're not going to make us sit through

another programme on East European cinema of the 1930s are you?" wailed Lloyd.

"This is even better," said Matthew, loading up the disc and switching on telly no. 6. "I thought I was getting a programme on East European cinema of the 1930s, but I'd forgotten to retune the recorder. It wasn't set to any actual TV channel. I should have recorded nothing but snowy static. Instead, ladies and gentlemen, I got this!"

For a few moments, the screen did indeed show nothing but snowy static. There was a flash, and a flicker. A series of lines like a giant barcode slid across the screen to reveal the words "Test Transmission". Then a picture of a packet of Wheetie Puffs appeared for exactly nine seconds, accompanied by a jingle which sounded as though it was being sung by a choir of mice with no talent:

> *Wheetie Puffs! Wheetie Puffs!*
> *They're made by science buffs!*
> *Wheetie Puffs! Wheetie Puffs!*
> *They never give you guffs!*
> *Wheetie Puffs!*
> *They're Wheetie sweetie to eat-y!*

The picture vanished, to be replaced by "Test Transmission End", then more static. Matthew switched off the TV and the video. Julie's eyes went all peculiar for a moment, in a way that would have given her mother a screaming fit.

"Good grief," said Lloyd. "That's the stupidest advert I've ever seen."

"Good grief," said Julie. "I ... I must have Wheetie Puffs!"

"Isn't it incredible?" said Matthew, handing Julie the open packet. "I've no way of knowing where it came from, but that has to be the greatest nine seconds of television ever made. You just *have* to have Wheetie Puffs. And then, when you've finished, you have to have them again. I went straight down to the corner shop after I saw it, and blew two weeks' pocket money. Thirty thousand years and two weeks I owe Mum now, but it was worth it. They're made by science buffs, you know."

He poured himself some more. Julie had already crammed half a dozen fistfuls into her mouth, and was reaching for the last of the unopened boxes.

"I don't get it," said Lloyd.

"Well, you're an artistic buffoon, aren't you?" said Matthew. "You wouldn't know quality work if it bit you on the bum. Whereas sensitive, cultured people like me and Julie – Oi, Custard, that's *mine*!"

They grappled on the floor. Lloyd had a number of ideas about things he'd like to have bite Matthew on the bum, but he kept them to himself. He stared out of the window and sighed. Julie won the fight by two thumps and

28

a nose twist, and clutched the now bat[...]
box of Wheetie Puffs to her chest.

"Wait a minute!" she said, shaking her head violently. "I'm desperate for these revolting things, and so are you. I don't care what that advert said, you can't just change your whole approach to sensible eating in nine seconds."

"But we have," said Matthew.

"I haven't," said Lloyd.

"It's distilled cinematic genius," said Matthew. "It's powerful, it's visionary, it's exactly what my films are all about."

Julie crammed in another couple of fistfuls. "No," she said. "It's weird. Something about that advert is very, very weird. Haven't you got any milk?"

Julie was, of course, completely right. To prove how right she was, we must turn our attention to a long, low building, situated just a couple of miles from Matthew's room. In the middle of this building was a large office. The furniture arranged around it was extremely expensive, and the shadows lurking in its every corner were extremely deep.

One wall was dominated by a darkened window overlooking a car park. The opposite wall was dominated by a series of framed photos and paintings, each of them showing a thin, dark-haired figure. The heavy wooden desk in the middle of the room was dominated by the thin, dark-haired figure himself, who sat behind it.

This was Mr Spite. No snake in the world had his large grey eyes, his pointed nose, his spidery fingers or his black suit and tie, and yet a snake was the first thing everyone who met him thought of. Podmore, his right-hand man, stood precisely where you'd expect him to.

"Your report?" said Mr Spite in a sharp, low voice.

"Yes, sir," said Podmore, blinking nervously behind his glasses. "The test transmission went out at approximately a quarter past three this morning, and was picked up clearly at our mobile receiver over three hundred miles away. A member of your staff watched it in progress. Um, that was Wilson, sir. You ordered him to volunteer or else meet with an unfortunate gardening accident, sir."

"And did Wilson encounter the full force of the experiment?"

"Yes, sir, he's onto his twenty-third jumbo economy pack now, sir. And has only been sick twice." Podmore felt a drip of sweat form on the back of his neck.

"Good," said Mr Spite slowly. "Have him meet with an unfortunate gardening accident anyway."

"Sir?" said Podmore. The drip of sweat paused, scared to go on without permission.

"We can't risk idle talk among the staff,"

said Mr Spite. He walked over to a large fish tank which stood next to an even larger set of bookshelves. "That test transmission was part of something I have personally dedicated vast quantities of time and money to. I will not allow its details to leak from the mouths of mere employees. See to Wilson, then order me a second volunteer, for the next test."

Podmore nodded slowly and left the room.

The light from the fish tank put an eerie pink glow into Mr Spite's eyes. He ran a long finger down the glass, in curling *S* shapes. The fish, dazzlingly coloured and weirdly shaped, darted to the corners of the tank with quick flicks of their tails. Mr Spite returned to his desk. He sat in his chair, not moving, hardly even breathing, listening to the silence.

EPISODE THREE

Matthew had changed his mind. The advert wasn't incredible, it was hugely scary. It was an outrageous infringement of his brain.

Cut to: the middle of next week. M. Bland eats secret stash of Wheetie Puffs! Then gets out of bed and eats non-secret stash of Wheetie Puffs for breakfast! On way to school, thumps junior kids to steal their money to buy Wheetie Puffs! M. Bland on slippery slope to rotten teeth and cruel nicknames! Because of Wheetie Puffs!

It had really been Julie who'd changed his mind for him, with all her talk of something weird going on, but he didn't like to admit it. What with the advert, and Julie's powers of persuasion, he wasn't sure how much of his mind was his to change any more.

Fortunately, the effects of the advert had lasted for only twenty-four hours. Matthew was relieved, not to say exhausted. Mum was delighted for two reasons: 1) it meant Matthew wouldn't be asking her to go down to the cash machine at the bank again and 2) by cutting all the Wheetie Value Tokens off the empty packets, she had enough Wheetie Points to send off for a new car.

However, the man at the corner shop was deeply upset. After Matthew had cleaned out his stock, he'd ordered a whole vanload of jumbo economy-sized boxes. Now that things were back to normal, his new vanload of unsold Wheetie Puffs filled the shop window from top to bottom, blocking out the light and being bought by absolutely no one.

On Monday morning, Matthew made his way to school lost in thought. He didn't pay any attention to the block of flats that would have been an ideal location for the spooky noises scene in his forthcoming film *Rabbit of Death*. He didn't read the card in the corner shop window saying "Wheetie Puffs: 2 for the price of 1!" He didn't notice when the Chemistry lab exploded and years 7, 8 and 9 had to be evacuated for forty minutes. The rest of the school day seemed to fly past in no more than a sentence.

By the time he got home, he had made a solemn vow never to go near that wretched advert ever again. Something creepy was going on, and he didn't want anything to do with it, in any way, at any time, for any reason, full stop, end of story.

Video no. 3 had recorded a second transmission. He'd forgotten that he'd set it searching for more adverts on Saturday night, while still in the grip of the Wheetie Puffs. Now the machine sat there, beneath a pile of movie magazines. The red "my disc is full" light that Matthew had rigged up was blinking away happily to itself.

No. He wasn't going to look. He had made a solemn vow. If sinister things were happening, the bad publicity might damage his career as a major director.

He switched on. The machine whirred into rewind. Static snowed heavily on telly no. 3, and then Matthew's eyes took on a glazed look, not unlike Mum's best china teapot. Nine seconds later, he was happy to find that he was still free of any desire to eat Wheetie Puffs. What he did have was a burning ambition to own …

"A complete set of Captain Zappo action figures!" he burbled to himself. "Captain Zappo, Tough Guy of Space! Own this galactastic range of toys, games and key rings! Batteries not included."

He slapped his hands to his mouth. No! Captain Zappo stuff was for girlies and weedy kids! It was *not* for young geniuses with bags of creativity and lots of admiring friends.

But... But... But he *wanted* a Zappo Destructo-Lab, with rotating dissection tool and free bucket of alien pus!

He ran out of his room screaming. He ran across the landing, down the stairs, through the hall, into the living-room, over Timothy's homework and landed with a wet splat in an X shape against the window. He let out a long, terrified wail that was something like "WooOO AaaarrrRRGGHHHH OooOOOoooooooOOOOO," only much worse.

"Matthew Bland!" cried Mum. "You've crinkled Timothy's homework!" She dropped the book she was reading and went all of a dither.

"It's perfectly all right, Mother," said Timothy. "I was only checking it through for spelling errors. Now I've confirmed that there aren't any I can print out a fresh copy on the computer."

"You hear that, Matthew?" said Mum. "I've got one son who thinks ahead. When was the last time you did duplicate homework in case someone ran over it screaming? Never, that's when. Too busy with your silly films. Get down from there."

Matthew peeled off the window and flopped backwards onto the sofa.

"Twenty-four hours," he wailed. "I can't last twenty-four hours. I have to have... Er,

Mum, dear Mum, whom I love with all my heart, um, how about making it thirty thousand years and six months?"

Mum's face went from being purple with rage to white with shock, and back again. Eventually, it settled down into a stormy red colour. "Wash your mouth out with soap and water, young man!"

"I could extend you some credit, Matthew," said Timothy, straightening his tie. "What is it you want to purchase?"

Matthew screwed his eyes up tightly. In his mind, the fearsome desire for a Zappo Ray Gun (with Blast Noise Selector) had a punch-up with the crushing embarrassment of asking for one. He was positively proud of himself when his mouth announced the winner:

"Oh, nothing."

"Your trouble," said Mum, "is that you never listen. Timothy offered to help you open a bank account."

"Mother's right, Matthew," said Timothy, in a calm tone of voice which was perfectly tuned to be not the slightest bit irritating. "If you'd invested your birthday money from Auntie Pam for the last three years in a personal fund management account, as I did, you'd now be able to buy a soundtrack mixing console. Or a set of spanners."

"See?" said Mum. The next thing she said was meant to fill Matthew's head with a deep sense of shame, but what it actually filled it with was an idea: "You never take advice when it's given to you."

Matthew's eyes popped open. What was it that movie company letter had said?

"Documentaries," he said quietly. That last letter had mentioned documentaries.

M. Bland waves to crowd! Reporters and TV news crews bite and kick each other in scrum to get microphone to him! "It was nothing," he says modestly. "All I needed was my camera, and my uncanny ability to expose evil-doing." Timothy tries to hide from prying media. "I waste my life, living in my brother's shadow," he confirms.

Matthew jumped off the sofa, ran over Timothy's homework, out of the living-room, through the hall, up the stairs, across the landing and into his room. His baggy old canvas props bag was soon loaded up with camera, spare batteries and the Captain Zappo toys page from Mum's mail order catalogue. For a few moments he considered phoning Lloyd, but in the end he decided that his mission was too important to delay. He'd just have to carry the bag himself.

Mum was sorting through the cupboard under the stairs. Matthew got to the front door and turned around in a way that would have looked really cool on a big screen, with a zoom-in on his round but square-jawed face.

"I'm off to the local TV station, Mum. No idea when I'll be back."

"Matthew Bland, you're banned from that building, and you know it! And I've got your tea in the oven."

"There's something darned weird goin' on, Mum," said Matthew, in a huge close-up with the light shining in his eyes. "I got my camera, I got a lead on a hot news story and I got interviews to do. Keep tea warm for me. I'm outta here."

Plan A: Present the adverts to the technical people at the TV station. Get their reactions to this terrifying evidence of mind control as part of a forthcoming *documentary* masterpiece *They Melted My Brain!*

Matthew strode across the car park towards the long, low building that housed Void TV.

Sudden thought: How did he know it wasn't Void TV who'd transmitted the adverts in the first place? How did he know they wouldn't have him arrested the minute he turned up, and sentenced to life in obscurity for criminal nosiness? How did he know they weren't already watching him from behind the darkened windows?

Plan B: Go home.

He paused. A stiff breeze rippled across the tarmac. The car park was nearly empty. Most of the station's employees had gone home for the evening. The sky was striped with orange and blue, like Lloyd's favourite jumper, and the sun sunk sulkily on the horizon.

He'd been here lots of times before, hadn't he? They'd always seemed like a nice bunch, hadn't they? Even the security guards who'd thrown him out onto the car park.

Plan C: Don't jump to conclusions.

He entered Reception, pausing only to free his bag from where it got caught in the huge, glass revolving door. He walked silently across the thick, spotless carpet, just as the receptionist was trying to sneak a chocolate biscuit out of the packet hidden under his chair. The receptionist was new to the job, and didn't recognize Matthew.

"Welcome to Void TV, how can I help you?" he said with a smile so big it almost fell off the sides of his face.

"Hallo," said Matthew. "I'm here to talk to your technical people."

The receptionist looked him up and down. His smile twitched slightly. "Do you have an appointment?"

"No, but I have this bag. In it are two recordings of vast significance which will send ripples of astonishment across the entire world, and which will without doubt blow their minds, their tops and their socks off."

"Not without an appointment they won't," said the receptionist. His rapidly vanishing smile was now on the point of dropping past the bottom of his chin.

They gave each other the hardest stares at their disposal. Matthew was sure he could smell chocolate.

"Who precisely do you wish to see?" growled the receptionist.

"I don't know," growled Matthew. "I've never been past Reception."

"You're a regular visitor? Name?"

"...Fred Smith."

The receptionist fumbled through a pile of papers attached to a clipboard behind his desk, and found a photo. His eyes snapped back to Matthew.

"Oooh, you liar. You're Matthew Bland and you're banned from this building!"

"No, that's my twin brother."

"It says here 'may pretend to be his twin brother.'" The receptionist pointed a shaky finger at one of the comfy chairs near the door. "Sit down! Wait there until I can call security to have you thrown out onto the car park! It says here 'has attempted to attend production meetings, replace broadcasts with his own material, eat cream cakes in the staff canteen...'" He was too shocked to go on.

"I can't help it if I've got initiative," said Matthew.

The receptionist pointed angrily. With a sigh, Matthew sank into the nearest chair, which was softer than Mr Prunely. The chair's arms were almost level with the top of his head.

The receptionist picked up the phone and hissed something urgent-sounding, dabbing his forehead with a hanky in an effort to keep calm. He replaced the receiver carefully, keeping an eye on Matthew at all times. He seemed like a nasty piece of work, this kid.

Matthew looked up at the displays of celebrity snapshots and TV memorabilia which were dotted around the walls. The warm, red light of the setting sun shone through the wide glass panels on each side of the revolving door, bathing Reception in a cosy glow. It was all very familiar, since he'd sat here so many times before – thinking, humming quietly, waiting to be thrown out onto the car park. Or rather, it was all very familiar except for one small bit above the receptionist's desk.

There, as usual, was the painting of the two blokes who looked like they were about to explode with wealth. They were labelled "Mr D. Ross & Mr Lew Kerr, founders of Void TV". Next to it, where two weeks before had hung a painting labelled "Cameramen Skipping Through the Forest", there was now a large, shadowy-coloured portrait labelled in thin black letters, "Mr U. B. Spite, Chairman and Head Overlord".

Matthew suddenly found himself thinking of a snake. A creepy sensation ran its finger in a zigzag down his spine. What had happened to the previous Chairman, that pleasant, grey-haired old chap who'd told him to get away from his car last Christmas?

There was an answer to Matthew's question, but it was far too horrible to talk about. There was no time to talk about it anyway, because something interesting was happening.

A tall, smartly dressed woman wearing an enormous hat and dark glasses entered the building. Once she'd pulled her hat from where it had got caught in the revolving door, she tipped it low over her face and approached the receptionist.

Matthew, thinking she looked dead suspicious, quietly took his camera from the bag. He recorded everything that went on, keeping the camera hidden behind the arm of the chair as much as possible. The receptionist had just finished his bit about having an appointment.

"Yes," said the woman, "Mr Spite is expecting me."

"And whom may I say you are?"

"Chief Executive of Wheetie Cereals Ltd."

Matthew almost dropped the camera, but being quite good at this undercover lark, he managed to keep his mouth shut and a blank expression on his face. The receptionist smiled and indicated that the Chief Executive of

Wheetie Cereals Ltd should take a seat. She headed for the chair next to Matthew.

"Not that one!" screamed the receptionist. The Chief Executive jumped half a metre off the carpet. "That boy's dangerous! Sit over there!"

The Chief Executive swerved and parked herself next to the door, through which was coming a short man in a long coat. His collar was turned up to mask his face. Once he'd got his tie out of the revolving door, he too approached the reception desk.

"Do you have an appointment?"

"I'm here to see Mr Spite. Tell him it's the Supreme Boss of Zappo Toys Inc."

Matthew almost dropped the camera again. This time, however good he was at this under-cover lark, nothing could prevent him from shouting out:

"Zappo Toys! Have you got a Captain Zappo Drive-Thru Spacewash Set going spare? Or one of those little Zappo Eater Monster action figures? Anything? I love them all! He's the Tough Guy of Space, you know!"

Instantly, Matthew was on his knees tug-ging at the Zappo man's coat. He was also thoroughly ashamed of himself that he'd let that advert get the better of him. The Zappo man tried to kick him away.

"I told you!" wailed the receptionist. "He's a menace! He's banned from this building!"

Security guards appeared from down a corridor. They gripped Matthew tightly and carried him out into the car park, pausing only to un-jam their peaked caps from the revolving door. They swung him backwards and forwards a couple of times, then launched him and his bagful of gear into the air. He landed with a painful thud on the tarmac.

"See ya, Matt," they called as they went back inside.

"See ya, guys," called Matthew, waving cheerily. Checking to make sure his camera was unharmed, he scrambled to his feet.

He had it! Vital evidence! The transmissions *had* come from Void TV! Those people from the companies who'd made the products in the adverts wouldn't be just innocently popping into the local TV station, would they? They *had* to know what was going on and so, logically, must this Mr Spite.

Matthew hurried off to share his discoveries with Lloyd and Julie, in time for the start of Episode Four.

EPISODE FOUR

Lloyd and Julie were amazed and terrified when they heard about Matthew's discoveries. Lloyd was more involved on the terrified side of things, and Julie tended to concentrate on being amazed. Matthew proudly showed them the footage he'd recorded at Void TV. He spent an evening giving them a dramatic and highly detailed reconstruction of events, and the breathtakingly daring part he'd played in them.

Once Lloyd and Julie had woken up, the three of them hit upon an idea to gather proper evidence of the adverts' effects on the human brain. Putting this idea into action involved a four-point plan.

1) Think up an experiment to be carried out on an unsuspecting audience in Room 12 of the Modern Languages Block.

2) Cut a small hole in the side of Lloyd's

school bag so that the lens of Matthew's camera could peep through.

3) Add the Wheetie Puffs advert to a copy of one of Matthew's most popular movies.

4) Print out a set of posters reading

You lucky people!
For <u>ONE</u> dinner break <u>ONLY!</u>
Back by <u>POPULAR DEMAND!</u>
The <u>DIRECTOR'S CUT</u> of Matthew Bland's
all—time classic of horror

See! Lloyd Martin <u>EATEN</u> by monsters!
Scream! As Julie Laburnam performs a
<u>HIDEOUS OPERATION!</u>
Not suitable for little kids or those of a
weedy disposition!
Don't miss it! (Or if you do, buy the video
from Bland, 7C)

Matthew pinned the posters up all around the school. Then he went all around the school again to write "Wednesday, Languages Block, Rm. 12" next to the second line on each one. A passing junior remarked that Martin Lloyd deserved to get eaten by monsters if he kept putting his name on back to front. Matthew ignored him. He was too busy waiting nervously for Wednesday.

On Wednesday morning, Matthew's school bag was heavier than normal because it concealed his camera equipment. His eyes were darting about all over the place because they concealed Point 1 of the plan.

The corner shop's window was still full of jumbo economy packs of Wheetie Puffs. Matthew didn't notice the new sign which said "Wheetie Puffs! FREE Jumbo Economy Pack with EVERY PURCHASE!"

Matthew, Lloyd and Julie were in Room 12 before the last echoes of the lunch break bell had bounced off the queue at the tuck shop. Lloyd's bag now had a circular hole in it, in line with Point 2 of the plan. They placed it on a desk at the back, where the camera could get a good view of the whole room.

Mr Nailshott arrived, wheeling the low metal trolley on which was balanced the precious departmental video player and TV. He unwound the machines' cables carefully.

"No smart remarks, Bland," he said, without looking up. "I'm not developing a taste for this particular brand of drivel. I drew the most stained exercise book from the bag in the Staff Room lottery. So I'm here as a forfeit. Got it?"

"Yes, sir," said Matthew. The three of them smiled innocently at him, and his moustache bristled like an exploding hedgehog. In his book, pupils smiling innocently meant other pupils committing some ghastly crime while he wasn't looking. However, in Matthew's book it simply meant that the three of them didn't want to give him any excuse to cancel the screening at the last minute.

Room 12 was soon packed out. Mr Prunely didn't come, the reason being that, oh dear, he was very sorry to find that he'd made a prior appointment to have his hair cut, so unfortunately he was unable to attend, but definitely next time. The real reason was that *Head Transplant* had given him the wobbles when it had first been shown at school, and he didn't want to spend another afternoon in the toilets crying into a length of loo roll.

Matthew knew the real reason, and made sure everyone in Room 12 knew it too, in order to create a relaxed atmosphere.

Half the audience were still chewing their lunch. Matthew thought this was pretty foolish, when they knew they were about to be scared out of their pants by scenes of unrelenting terror. However, he reminded himself that his masterpiece was but a simple lure. The real point of the screening would be over before Lloyd had even had all his blood drained out by Julie the mad scientist.

The lights went off. Whistles and rude noises.

"Belt up!" yelled Mr Nailshott.

Then, in line with Point 3 of the plan, it was upon them! Without warning, Matthew's specially edited recording began with the first of the test adverts.

Silence. Dozens of pairs of eyes went all peculiar for a moment. Matthew and Julie kept their fingers jammed tightly in their ears, and their faces pressed painfully against a poster on the back wall depicting "The Cheeses Of France".

There were murmurings in the audience as the advert finished. There were whispers and suppressed cries as the opening titles of *Head Transplant* appeared. It was Mr Nailshott who finally broke the silence.

"Wheetie Puffs!" he screamed, then coughed loudly in embarrassment.

"Wheetie Puffs!" screamed most of the audience.

Lloyd still didn't get it.

Room 12 was suddenly unpacking itself. Mr Nailshott abandoned his TV and video, and fled. By the time Dr Heather Foulpest *(Julie Laburnum)* injected hapless passing tourist Vic *(Matthew Bland)* with Formula Z death inducer *(washing-up liquid mixed with a bit of green paint)*, most of the audience had pretended to have a sudden attack of the wobbles, and rushed out. Only five remained in their seats.

"Wow, Bland," called one of them, "this must be one hell of a movie."

Matthew and Julie unplugged their ears.

"Well?" said Matthew.

"I still don't get it," said Lloyd.

49

"No, but did you get it on camera?"

Lloyd reached into the bag and switched off the camera. He gave it a little pat. Matthew slapped him on the back. "Hah! Perfect!" Lloyd flinched, and wanted to say something about his bag now being rather less than perfect, but didn't.

"Five people left," said Julie. "They must be immune, like Lloyd. So judging by this experiment, I'd guess it affects about ninety per cent of the population. It has to be caused by some sort of hypnotic signal. They say there are some people hypnotism doesn't work on, and it's the same with these adverts."

"Hmm, so it's not just an intelligence thing, then?" said Matthew, watching Lloyd trying to scrunch up the lens hole in his bag and join it all back together with a stapler.

On the TV screen, hero and novelist Colin Stark *(Lloyd Martin)* was being eaten alive by Dr Foulpest's mutant monster *(Matthew Bland, with the assistance of the hairy rug from the spare room)*. The audience of five were so bored they were on the point of pretending to have a sudden attack of the wobbles too.

Meanwhile, Mr Nailshott and the rest of the audience were now firmly under the control of the advert. They raced for Super Save, the nearest supermarket, dribbling slightly and searching their pockets for cash.

"I think we've got enough evidence to take to the police now," said Julie. "With what we've just recorded we can prove that Void TV are conducting mind control experiments, and with what you got the other day we can more or less prove that the Wheetie Puffs and Captain Zappo people are in on it too."

"Go to the police?" hissed Matthew, shocked. "How am I going to make my blockbuster documentary that way? I need footage of those responsible at Void TV acting in a highly suspicious manner, I need tearful interviews with those whose lives have been ruined by Wheetie Puffs —"

"Matthew," gasped Julie, "are you putting your documentary before the mental safety of the entire population of the world?"

"Yes," said Matthew. "I think our next step should be to bunk off double P.E. this afternoon, stake out Void TV and watch for anything incriminating."

"OK," said Julie.

"I haven't got double P.E.," said Lloyd. "I've got a Chemistry test."

"Are you going to pass it?" said Matthew.

"Probably not," said Lloyd, sadly. "I spent the time I should have been studying doing screams for your sound effects library."

"Well, it won't matter if you miss it, then,

will it?" said Matthew.

*M. Bland & co. synchronize watches. L.
Martin has no watch – J. Custard draws one
on his wrist showing correct time. Put on big
coats and dark glasses. "Don't go, brave
young heroes!" calls Nailshott, mouth full of
Wheetie Puffs. "'Tis most grievously dangerous!" They go anyway. M. Bland wins medal
for services to film-making.*

Even in the middle of the day, long, dark shadows crawled around Mr Spite's office, like the
fingers of a sleeping giant. Mr Spite's own fingers tapped slowly and silently on the polished
surface of his desk. He didn't look up from
The Encyclopedia of Sharks, which was open
in front of him at a page of gruesome colour
photos. His voice was low, quiet and precise.

"Please explain yourself, Podmore."

Podmore was relieved that his trousers had
just enough spare room in them to conceal the
shaking of his right leg. He cleared his throat
awkwardly. "The technician supervising the
test transmissions may possibly have forgotten
to scramble the signal, sir. It could, maybe,
perhaps have been picked up locally, sir.
Purely by accident."

"And what leads him to think such a thing,
Podmore?"

"He was in Super Save at lunchtime, sir."

Mr Spite's left eyebrow arched. He looked

up. "Super Save, Podmore?"

"Yes, sir. It's all here in his report. I'll read it to you, sir.

"'*REPORT BY TECHNICIAN X-7, TECHNICAL SECTION 3 – EVEN MORE THAN TOP SECRET. At 12:41 pm today, Wednesday, I was walking in a north-easterly direction into town. The purpose was for the buying of my dinner, namely an egg sandwich. The egg sandwich in question being from my favourite supermarket, Super Save.*'

"I'll skip the next bit, sir," said Podmore. "It's mostly about mayonnaise and wholemeal bread." He continued from further down the page.

"'*The time was now exactly 12:43 pm. I entered Super Save from the High Street, heading westerly. I turned and moved northerly, avoiding the yoghurt. I did not in any way buy any of the yoghurt. This was on account of what it does to my intestines, namely makes them all runny.*

"'*It was then that I observed a group of school-style young persons. With them was a man with a moustache like a toothbrush, whom I took to be their teacher. I noticed them on account of they all trampled me to the floor.*

"'*At first, I had terrible fears that they were trying to beat me to the egg sandwiches. However, with my ears I observed them crying out* for Wheetie Puffs.

"'This had the effect of making me suspicious. Painfully, I crawled in a north-westerly direction, and observed the young persons grabbing every last packet of Wheetie Puffs from the shelves. Some of them continued on to the checkouts. However, most of them ripped the packets apart and scoffed the lot there and then.

"'The teacher had now become completely barmy, on account of he had failed to get a packet for himself. However, he spotted a mini fun-size pack in the trolley of an old lady. The old lady hit him with her umbrella a total of six times to get him out of her trolley.

"'I observed that these young persons and their teacher were behaving in the same way as caused by the Void TV test transmission, on account of the drooling and the running up and down. I worked out in my brain that they had seen the transmission in an unauthorized and not-allowed manner. At this point, I turned and went south-westerly, back to Void TV. I have missed my dinner, and have not had an egg sandwich. THE END.'

"He came immediately to report the incident, straight away, at once," stammered Podmore.

Mr Spite was silent for a moment. His fingers paused in midair. "He tried to do the right thing, Podmore. Reporting a breach of security like that."

"Yes, sir, he's a good man, sir, he's very worried about it, sir."

"Reward him, Podmore. With a holiday. The Amazon jungle is beautiful at this time of year. He'll enjoy himself there. What a pity the place is so full of … reptiles, and … poisonous spiders. See to it."

"Y-yes, sir," said Podmore. His other leg had started shaking too.

Mr Spite closed the book on his desk. He rose silently, and replaced it on the shelf behind him. "Bring the schedule forward by one week," he said, stepping forward so that the thin red line of his mouth emerged from the shadows. "We begin tonight. And one other thing, Podmore. Those children in the supermarket cannot all have seen our first test transmission by chance. Therefore someone recorded it, and showed it to them. They will have been searching for the nearest available supply of Wheetie Puffs. Therefore they must have come from the nearest school. You will go to that school, Podmore, and you will find out who has been holding public screenings of top secret material. I'd like to meet them."

Burger Shed was the worst fast food restaurant in town. Usually, it was only visited by teenagers who thought they looked trendy holding a soggy Double-Decker Shedder, and little kids who'd worn their parents out with three weeks of continuous whining. The likes of Matthew, Lloyd and Julie never normally set foot in the place, but they went there that afternoon because, from its front window, you could get a clear view of the comings and goings at Void TV.

"Oh, go on," said Matthew.

"I am not lending you any money," said Lloyd through a mouthful of chips. "It's not my fault your mum's banned you from having any more cash till you're twenty-one."

"I shouldn't bother, Matt," said Julie. She was concentrating with screwed-up eyes on a huge limousine, which was purring gracefully through Void TV's main gates. "Quite apart from the fact that this place has an appalling record for encouraging inhumane farming methods, those chips are packed full of preservatives. They'll outlive all three of us."

A small knot of girls from 9C had arrived, and were busily weighing up the pros and cons of each flavour of milk-shake. Lloyd gasped and whipped off his glasses.

"So much for bunking off," mumbled Matthew sadly. "We've seen nothing suspicious, and if 9C are here it must be past going-home time anyway."

Lloyd clutched Matthew's arm. "Dawn Gardner's with them!" he hissed. "W-where is she now?"

"With your eyesight," said Matthew, "I'd guess she's the black and white blob next to the red blob." It was at times like this he deeply regretted causing Lloyd's irrational fear of contact lenses with his stories about burrowing eyeball germs.

"Don't let her see me," hissed Lloyd, turning a colour that would have made a post box go "Oo, aren't you red".

"She won't even recognize you without your most distinguishing feature," said Matthew. "Nobody does."

"Just don't do anything to embarrass me," whispered Lloyd urgently.

"Oi, Dawn!" shouted Matthew at the top of his voice. A slim girl with short dark hair turned around. Lloyd dived under the table. Matthew took the opportunity to stuff all the chips off Lloyd's plate into his mouth.

Julie was too busy shaking with excitement to worry about all that. She had spotted a tall, elegantly dressed figure getting out of the limousine and gliding into the building, pausing only to unhook her sunglasses from the revolving door.

"It's Laburnum Groves!" she cried. "She must be filming something here!"

Laburnum Groves was her favourite film star. She admired Ms Groves's acting, she adored Ms Groves's good looks and sophistication and she bitterly envied Ms Groves's exotic first name (which of course she'd already borrowed to use in Matthew's movies). She let out a squeal of delight, which made Matthew jump.

He shrugged his shoulders. Both his friends had just had nice surprises, but was there any chance whatsoever of him finding a brand new special effects workstation left lying around in the street? He didn't think so.

They went home. Julie spent the evening writing in her diary. Lloyd spent the evening composing a poem. Matthew spent the evening cataloguing his collection of lens filters and spraying deodorant on the pile of dirty clothes in his wardrobe.

Luckily, neither they nor their families ever watched the TV comedy show *Whoops! Vicar*. Unluckily, millions of people did.

At 8:15 pm, just after Rev. Pratt had hilariously got his head stuck in a toilet and the caption "End Of Part One" had faded away, a full thirty-second version of Void TV's Wheetie Puffs advert was transmitted across the nation.

All night, out there in the darkness, there were screams and crunchy noises.

EPISODE FIVE

"...And with the time coming up to news time, it's time for the news on Radio Groove, and here with the news is our news man, Kevin Headline!"

"Thanks, Dave. The top story this morning is Wheetie Puffs! Yup, the nation wakes up to Wheetie mania! We've always thought they were the yukkiest cereal in the shops, but following last night's mega-successful advertising campaign, they're suddenly all the rage! Don't get it myself, but hey, I'm a cornflakes kind of guy. Back to you, Dave... Dave, what's that you're eating?..."

It was getting to be a habit for Matthew to hurry to school, lost in thought. Ever since he'd woken up, he'd been hearing strange sounds out in the street. Those strange sounds, mingled with cries of "They're Wheetie sweetie to eat-y!" and "Gimme that packet!" had given him worse shivers than last winter's flu. Clearly, Void TV's evil schemes were getting underway fast.

Hideous mind bandits stand poised to take over the whole country! he thought to himself, as he fought off a gang of toddlers who thought he smelt of puffed wheat. *Nearly anyone could be forced to think nearly anything! About any old rubbish. Today, breakfast cereal, tomorrow, brussels sprouts! Or Bogstop United! Or some mad dictator out to rule the world!*

He hurried on. He didn't notice the new sign in the corner shop window saying, "Wheetie Puffs: beat the shortage! Only £197.50 a cupful! Limit one per customer."

By the time he got to school, he had three questions. Firstly, why was the place half empty? Answer: Most people were out searching for you know what. Secondly, was his special edition of *Head Transplant* still safely tucked away in Room 12? Answer: No. Thirdly, when were these wretched toddlers going to get lost? Answer: Once they heard the crunchy noises coming from the school canteen.

It was the answer to the second question which concerned him most. He'd hidden the disc behind a pile of copies of *France: The Language, The Country* on Mr Nailshott's bookshelf. As soon as he came dashing into Room 12 and skidded to a halt, he could see that the books were scattered across the room and that the disc was gone.

He got an empty feeling in his stomach which had nothing to do with only having had time for two plates of beans on toast at breakfast. When Julie and Lloyd arrived and also saw that the books had been flung into fluttering heaps, they got empty feelings too.

"Oh no," said Julie, out of breath from running.

"Too right," said Lloyd, out of breath from trying to keep up with Julie. "Those books might be torn, or anything."

"I mean the disc," said Julie. "You know what I think's happened, Matt?"

"Yes," said Matthew, "my fans will do anything to get hold of a copy of *Head Transplant*."

"No," said Julie. "It means Void TV are on to us!"

Matthew's empty feeling dived into his legs and took his stomach with it. "Oh, crumbs," he whispered. "You're right, it'll be the test transmissions the disc's been stolen for. I let a whole classroom and a teacher see that advert. Void TV must have spotted them on the rampage. It wouldn't take a complete brainbox to follow the trail back here."

"They'll know about our experiment," said

Julie, in a trembly voice. "And if they know about our experiment, they'll know we're gathering evidence against them."

Huge close-up of M. Bland! Bead of sweat glistens on forehead! Eyes widen as avalanche of fear cascades through brain! (But still manages to look really heroic in a dashing, creative genius kind of way.)

"And if they know about us," said Matthew quietly, "they'll know where I live. Our addresses are all in the Headmaster's office. They could lure his secretary away from her filing cabinets."

"If she watched TV last night, all they'd need is a bowl of Wheetie Puffs," said Julie, even more quietly.

"Quick!" yelled Matthew, suddenly snapping into action. "They'll be raiding my room! They'll take every shred of evidence! They'll be so jealous of my movies they'll probably take them too! Come on!"

The three of them had no trouble sneaking back out through the school gates and off to Matthew's house, since there were very few adults around any of the main buildings that morning. They were amazed at how popular *Whoops! Vicar* obviously was with teachers. They were also amazed at how most people seemed to be taking this whole Wheetie Puffs thing in their stride.

"Don't they think it's peculiar, suddenly

wanting something they've always hated?" gasped Matthew as they ran past the bus stop.

"Perhaps not thinking it's peculiar is part of the hypnotic signal," gasped Julie as they passed the block of flats by the petrol station.

"I think they're just used to it," gasped Lloyd as they passed the crowd squashing into the corner shop. "My auntie buys things whenever there's a fluffy kitten in the advert. And there's no hypnotic signal in those ones."

"Not that we know about," mumbled Matthew, under what little breath he had left.

The whole morning was rapidly becoming one huge piece of bad news. No sooner had they arrived at Matthew's house than they were getting those empty feelings again.

The front door was slightly ajar. Matthew was sure he hadn't left it like that. Mum wouldn't have left it like that, because she was always frightened of someone running off with the china poodle she kept next to the hall mirror. Timothy wouldn't have left it like that, because he was Timothy.

For a moment, the three of them looked at each other. Then they hurried inside and Matthew bounded up the stairs. Half a minute later, he bounded down them again.

"Too late," he said. "They've got everything. They've even got my camera!"

"That's not all they've got," said Julie sadly, holding a neatly printed note that had been sticky-taped to the china poodle. She read it out loud:

Dearest Matthew,

Hope you are well. Your mother and brother are paying me an extended visit. This will, I'm afraid, become a permanent one if you say anything to anyone, or continue your investigations into certain private matters.

With love,
An anonymous friend

"That is IT!" cried Matthew. "We're going to the police!"

"'*P.S. Or go to the police*,'" read Julie.

Matthew flopped onto the bottom stair. The empty feeling had been replaced by something that was trying very hard to leak out of his eyes.

"I am not going to be silenced!" he said angrily. "They're not going to threaten me or my mum and get away with it!... Timothy I'm still thinking about."

"They can't threaten him either!" cried Julie.

"No, I suppose not," sighed Matthew.

He looked up at them. He won his battle with the eye-leaking thing.

"I'm going to infiltrate Void TV," he said, "and I'm going to get that evidence back. I'm also going to be very careful not to be spotted. Mum will kill me if she gets murdered. And

I can't ask you two to come with me. If they know about me, they know about you, and they might go after your families as well."

Julie sat on the stair beside him. "Of course we're coming with you," she said.

"Yeah," said Lloyd. "We've been splattered with fake blood, eaten alive and failed Physics exams because of you. Surely you don't think this is going to stop us?"

Matthew felt a bit odd saying what he said next, but he said it anyway. "You're, um... You're good friends, you know... Let's go and kick their teeth in!"

"Yeah!" they cried.

"Not literally, of course," he added hurriedly.

"Fooooooorrrget it, sunshine!"

"Please! Please, oh please, let me in!" wailed the clown.

"No," growled the security guard.

"I'll get you a free balloon!"

"No."

"I'll do my funny hedgehog routine, live in your own home!"

"No."

"But I'm Big Bob the Bouncing Clown!" he yelled, going redder than his plastic comedy nose.

"You might be a terrorist in disguise," growled the guard.

"A terrorist?" screeched Bob. "What kind of stupid terrorist dresses up and pretends to be Big Bob the Bouncing Clown?"

"Your kind, obviously."

Bob's enormous comedy trousers shook with rage. His squirting comedy flower jittered on the lapel of his polka-dotted comedy jacket. He tried to speak calmly, and nearly managed it. "I am a leading celebrity. I am due to record *Big Bob's Big Bonanza Quiz* in ten minutes! I demand you let me in!"

"No."

"For the love of God!" howled Bob. "You've known me for eighteen years, Frank!"

"No security card, no getting in. Now push off."

Bob's green comedy hair flapped in all directions as he ran away screaming.

"That is a really tough security guard," gasped Lloyd.

He, Matthew and Julie were hiding behind a battered old van full of lighting equipment. They were outside the side entrance to Void TV, the one used by most of the scene shifters, make-up artists, cameramen and other studio staff. The security guard stood immobile in front of a large metal door, his arms at his sides, his mouth set in an upside-down *U*. Even his uniform stood to attention.

"Yeah," said Matthew, "that's Fearsome

Frank. He's hurled me into the rubbish bins a couple of times. We're old friends. Mind you, there's not normally a guard on this entrance. There's a coded lock for getting in and out. And a surveillance camera."

"They must be really worried about security," said Julie.

"Could be," said Matthew. "I'm world famous around here. They know they've got to be pretty quick to catch the leading movie director of the early twenty-first century."

"I was thinking more along the lines of keeping their little mind control secret under wraps," said Julie.

"So how do we get in?" said Lloyd impatiently.

"I have absolutely no idea," sighed Matthew.

A slow but steady stream of people were now arriving at the side entrance, chattering excitedly. Some of them wore knitted cardigans, and many of them had nicely polished shoes. Matthew reckoned they were the most boring looking crowd he'd ever seen.

"Must be the audience for *Big Bob's Big Bonanza Quiz*," he said. "Yeah, look, they've all got tickets."

Fearsome Frank closely inspected the large gold-coloured papers they all held. Then he checked their identities against the photo-IDs they'd had to submit in advance. Then he checked their identities again, by telephone with their bank managers. Then he let them through the door in single file, no talking, no spitting on company property.

"That's it," said Lloyd. "We can sneak in pretending to be one of them."

"Not without tickets, we can't," said Matthew.

"I know," said Julie, with an I've-got-a-brilliant-idea expression suddenly hugging her face like a favourite teddy bear. "The effects of last night's advert won't have worn off yet. We can use Void TV's own weapon against them."

She bounded out from their hiding place. Matthew and Lloyd followed, keeping a wary eye on Fearsome Frank.

"Hey, Matt!" cried Julie, making sure she was loud enough to be heard by everyone. "You know what first prize in the quiz is?"

"Eh?" said Matthew, not catching on at all.

Julie took a deep breath. "A year's supply of Wh—"

Her last word and a half were drowned out by the stampede. The crowd knocked Frank off his feet, yelling and waving their arms about for no very good reason. Frank was three corridors and a staircase away before he could reach the emergency panic button sewn into his haircut.

By then, our heroes were inside the building,

and wondering which way to go. They moved off in the opposite direction to the one in which Frank had been carried. Before them was a long, echoing walkway, off which branched several more long, echoing walkways. Thick power cables snaked around the floor in several places. At one junction, a tall pile of old film cans teetered alarmingly, and half a dozen military costumes were draped over a large wicker basket marked "Property VTV plc." Above them, the ceiling was a mass of pipes, wires and connections, punctuated with long, fluorescent lights. They bathed the bare, whitewashed walls in an eerie glow.

"Don't you know your way around?" whispered Julie.

"I've never got past Reception before, have I?" whispered Matthew helplessly.

"We'll have to decide quickly," murmured Lloyd. "They could be onto us any minute."

"Quite right," said Matthew, as confidently as his terror-stricken voice would allow. "Julie, you track down Mum and Timothy. Lloyd, you and I will locate the source of the mind control experiments, gather any available evidence and slip out from under the noses of staff and security guards."

"Can't I track down Mum and Timothy?" said Lloyd.

"No, you can't. When the good guys get caught in spy movies, it's always the softer one who gets shouted at and interrogated first. Julie's tougher than school beefburgers, so I'm sticking with you, Softy."

Lloyd muttered about other things he'd like Matthew to stick to. The three of them split up, and hurried away down two different corridors.

At exactly the same moment, Mum and Timothy were wishing that they could hurry away somewhere too. A couple of hours ago, they'd been standing next to the china poodle in the hall back home. Timothy had been informing Mum of his timetable for the day when masked intruders had suddenly forced paper bags over their heads and bundled them into a car. The next thing they knew, they were being flung to the floor, and had pulled off the paper bags to find themselves in a tiny, wooden room with a heavy, wooden door. There were no windows and no furniture. The only light came from a single bulb, just above their heads.

"I told him!" wailed Mum. "I told him a million times, all this film rubbish would lead to his poor mother being kidnapped by murderous thugs! But did he listen?"

"There, there, Mother," said Timothy, straightening his tie. "Never fear, for I have formulated an escape plan, based on various elements of my school studies."

"Oh, Timothy," said Mum lovingly, "at least I have one son who can get his mother out of a dangerous situation."

Timothy crouched down, took his paper bag, flattened it out, and slipped it under the door in a position directly under the lock. Then he took a new, sharp pencil from his pocket, and poked it into the lock mechanism.

"Our captors have foolishly left the key in the door," he said. "All I have to do is push it out with the pencil. It falls onto the paper bag and I pull it under the door. Hey presto, we can escape."

He pushed the pencil. The key fell out. KA-DOINK! It bounced off the paper bag and out of reach.

"Ah," said Timothy.

"Oh, Timothy," wailed Mum.

EPISODE SIX

"...*Thanks, Dave. Top news story this late morning time on Radio Groove is free tellies! Yup, them guys down at Void TV are so darned great that they've announced they're giving away a free goggle box to anyone who wants one! A spokesman for Void TV said 'We just want people to enjoy Void TV programmes, and the adverts that appear during them.' An old lady in the local shopping centre said, 'What lovely, lovely people. Now I can have one in the toilet, and never miss my favourite episodes of* Whoops! Vicar.*' Here at Radio Groove we say, FAB! Just don't let it make you miss our chart rundown, OK? Back to you, Dave...*"

Julie had never been so utterly delighted in her entire life. She hadn't found Mum and Timothy, nor had she found out that her parents had been fooling her all these years about her surname. She had found Laburnum Groves.

Studio 2 was filled with the sounds of people shouting, hammers hammering and saws sawing. Huge, dazzling lights, hanging from the high ceiling on long, extending runners, were being manoeuvred into various positions. Production assistants with clipboards ran one way looking frantic, while more production assistants with clipboards ran the other way looking even more frantic. The studio itself was about the size of an aircraft hangar, but from where Julie was standing most of it was hidden from sight by the sets around which everyone was working.

Julie could see the interior of a palace, the interior of a grubby-looking stables, and the interior of a cottage. She could also see the back of another interior which had pieces of Void TV paper pasted to it, and which was marked with enormous numbers slapped on in black paint. The sets were slightly smaller than real rooms would have been. All the details and props suddenly stopped when they got near to the edges, marking the limits of what the cameras would be pointed at. It all fitted in with what she remembered of Matthew's series of lectures on modern television production techniques.

And there, sitting in the middle of the palace

set, was Laburnum Groves. She was wearing a billowing eighteenth-century costume and sipping mineral water from a plastic carton through a straw.

"She's … she's just brilliant," thought Julie.

Julie took her eyes off Ms Groves long enough to pluck a copy of the script from a nearby table, and read: "*Scent & Stupidity – A Historical Romance* by Wyndham Bagg. Cast: Mr Ferret – Hammond Eggs, Miss Dashboard – Laburnum Groves…"

It was really her. She was really here. Her biggest fan was really here too.

When Julie looked up, Ms Groves had finished sipping her mineral water and was busy spitting it back out again. She squeaked loudly and fluttered her fingers at a young man wearing headphones and a dopey smile.

"This is warm!" she squealed. "Warm! When I say straight from the fridge, I mean straight from the fridge. I don't mean straight from the fridge, pausing under a heat lamp for twenty minutes on the way, do I?"

"No, Ms Groves," said the assistant. "I'll change it at once."

"It's too late now!" piped Ms Groves. "My throat is awash with warmth! Get me ice, boy, quickly! That's 'quickly', meaning some time *before* I die of thirst. Oh, Arthur, darling Arty!" She had shifted her attention to the director, a tall man with grey hair and a

74

chunky jumper, who was walking past. "Arthur, you *have* reconsidered my request, haven't you?"

The director picked nervously at the waistband of his jeans. "Labby, sweetheart, they didn't have mobile phones in 1797. You can't take a call in the middle of the banquet scene."

"My agent is getting me a role in the next *Batman* movie!" squeaked Ms Groves. "Hollywood will want an answer!"

"Well, they can't have one in the middle of the banquet scene!" yelled the director angrily.

Ms Groves's face became perfectly still for a moment, her large and rather beautiful eyes staring at him, aflame with rage. She stood up suddenly. She looked tall and graceful, exactly as she had done during her role as Madeleine Warmly, the wronged heiress in *Roses of the House of Gold*. It was a performance Julie had studied closely for her own role as Mitzi Steel, the mutant healthcare worker in *Swamp Nurse*.

"You!" cried Ms Groves, pointing at Julie. "Bring Snoozle!" She marched off the set, nose held high.

Snoozle, her Yorkshire terrier, finished chewing up the seat of a priceless eighteenth-century chair, yapped loudly and scurried over to Julie. His little legs scuttered on the studio floor. He jumped into Julie's arms and wet all down the front of her blouse.

"Come on! Come on!" called Ms Groves, waltzing towards her dressing-room.

Julie followed, meekly. Snoozle wriggled and yapped. Ms Groves flung open the dressing-room door and flung it shut again behind Julie.

"Put Snoozle in his basket," squeaked Ms Groves, arranging herself in front of the mirror at her make-up table and slapping cream all over her face, "and fetch him a bowl of milk. Skimmed! You do know what 'skimmed' means, don't you? Not full fat, not semi-skimmed! Skimmed! And then tell Arthur that I'm not coming out until he's called my agent. And then get me a fresh copy of the script. Mine is wrapped around that simply dreadful apology for a salmon sandwich they gave me this morning. And then call my limousine round to the main entrance. I'm going home early. I have a quite ghastly headache coming on."

"She's … she's a complete cow," thought Julie.

By now, Ms Groves's face was totally free of make-up. How strange she looked without it. How … average.

"She's … she's no prettier than me," thought Julie.

And how odd Ms Groves seemed once she'd kicked off the thick platform shoes she wore under her costume. How … short.

"She's … she's no taller than me either,"

thought Julie.

"What on earth are you staring at, you ridiculous girl?" squealed Ms Groves.

"Nothing," said Julie, gobsmacked, "nothing at all."

Ms Groves flung her soft, silky wig onto the make-up table, scratched her remarkably average hair, and went to have a lie down.

Meanwhile, Matthew and Lloyd were having no more success than Julie. They'd wandered around for a while, suspecting they were lost. Now they had come to a stop, absolutely sure they were lost. The corridor they were in looked exactly like all the other corridors they'd been in, and none of them seemed to lead anywhere in particular.

"We've got to find where they're running the experiments from, and quick," said Lloyd, his voice shivery with fright. "Fearsome Frank and the rest of the security guards could be here any minute."

"I know, I know," said Matthew nervously. "Just let me think."

Approaching them down the corridor was a man in glasses, a crumpled shirt, and a pair of trainers which made the inside of a dustbin look clean and respectable. He whistled tunelessly as he flipped through a script.

"I've thunk," said Matthew. "Lloyd, I want you to stop this chap, real casual-like, and interrogate him."

"Why me?"

"You stop him, maybe ask him the time, possibly. But be subtle. Be devious. Act natural. Engage him in conversation. Ask intelligent questions, the answers to which may give us clues to the location of the experiments."

As the man passed them, Lloyd stepped boldly out in front of him.

"Could you tell me where the mind control experiments are, please?"

"Sure," said the man, turning and pointing his script in the opposite direction. "Down there, turn left, third on the right."

"Thanks," said Lloyd. The man went about his business.

If Matthew had been starring in a not-very-good comedy film at that moment, his eyes would have bounced out on stalks, accompanied by a loud "BOING!" noise. As it was, he settled for gasping, "Lloyd, you're almost as talented as I am."

Down there, turn left, third on the right was a sliding black door covered in coded entry systems, security cameras, emergency alarms and a really enormous padlock.

"Is this it?" said Lloyd.

"No, it's where the cleaner keeps his squirty polish," said Matthew. "Of course this is it. And there's no way we're going to get inside with this lot activated. I bet those cameras have picked us up already."

"We'd better get out of here!" cried Lloyd. His eyes darted left and right. It only made him feel sick, but it was the sort of thing he felt he ought to be doing at a time like this.

"We can't afford to be the centre of attention," said Matthew, "so we need a diversion of some kind. More to the point, we need to have this door opened for us."

He looked around the walls, the floor, the ceiling. Amid the mass of wires and pipes above them was the fat red nozzle of a fire sprinkler. Beside it was a small grey box through which a number of cables were routed. He beckoned Lloyd over to him, got him to stand directly under the box, then clambered up him to reach the cables.

"Ammff chunnpee phnee," grunted Lloyd, with Matthew's left shoe wedged between his jaws.

"It's perfectly simple," said Matthew. "If the article I read in last month's issue of *TV Production Smartypants* was accurate, cables like these are likely to be carrying sound and pictures between studios. Disconnect the equipment, but leave the power on, and the signal booster in this grey box will very quickly overheat."

Before Lloyd could free his mouth, in order to shout "No! That's horribly dangerous!" Matthew grabbed all but one of the cables tightly, and ripped them down.

There was a flash of electric sparks. Smoke began to pour from the box. The lights went out, to be replaced by emergency red lighting set into the floor. The sprinkler gurgled and hissed. An instant later, freezing cold water fired in all directions.

A calm, electronic voice echoed down the corridor: "Evacuate Technical Section 3. Possible fire hazard. All personnel to fire exits."

There was a series of heavy clangs and clicks as the locks on the black sliding door disengaged. It hummed open. Three technicians dashed out, almost knocking over Matthew and Lloyd in their hurry to escape.

"Evacuate Corridor A-41," said the voice.

"Brilliant!" yelled Matthew above the noise of the rushing water. "Quick, we've only got minutes before we're discovered! Inside!"

They jumped through the doorway and found themselves surrounded by TV screens, editing equipment and computers. Drips from their soaking wet clothes and hair formed rippling puddles at their feet.

"It's like your room," said Lloyd. "Only nice."

"I think I'm in love," sighed Matthew. "All this lovely gear – and look what they're using it for!" He quickly glanced over the machinery, identifying most of it from the catalogues he read under the bed covers at night. He hopped onto a swivel chair in front of a particularly large and cool-looking computer. "From here, we can download the programs that generate the hypnotic signal. I think."

At that moment, the sprinkler in the corridor switched off. Water drizzled down the walls and the normal lights came back on.

"They know it's a trick," cried Matthew.

"Hurry up, then!" yelled Lloyd in a voice like a hamster being sat on.

Matthew knocked over a carefully stacked pile of computer discs as he fumbled to load one into the machine. They scattered and clattered over the floor. He tapped nervously at the keyboard.

It was weirdly quiet outside. Just *drip, drip, drip*.

The disc clunked into place in the computer. Matthew found the files he needed and clicked on "Save to Disc".

"Thank goodness this thing isn't password protected," he whispered.

WuuAAAAAA! WuuAAAAAA!

A deafening alarm sounded. All the screens in the room turned red. The calm electronic voice echoed down the corridor: "Security alert, code one. Password omitted. Section shut-down in force—"

"Run!" shouted Matthew.

Lloyd was already leaping through the doorway.

"Start data transfer and room termination," said the voice.

Lloyd slipped on the wet floor of the corridor and landed against the opposite wall with a thud. The sound of the alarm made his head throb. He turned to look for Matthew –

"Room termination begins."

– and caught sight of him heading for the door as it whizzed shut in his face. Lloyd scrambled to his feet and hammered against it as hard as he could. On top of the alarm, he could now hear the sound of pounding boots.

"Matt! MAAAATTTTT!"

At exactly the same moment, Mum and Timothy were pounding on the walls of their tiny prison.

"It's no good!" wailed Mum. "Nobody can hear us! But will Matthew feel guilty for the rest of his life, knowing what dreadful torment he's put his poor mother through? No!"

"There, there, Mother," said Timothy, adjusting his shirt cuffs. "Never fear, for I have formulated another escape plan, based on various elements of my training as school athletics champion."

"Oh, Timothy," said Mum lovingly, "at least I have one son who's not a lazy good-for-nothing."

Timothy stood with his back to the wall and made mental calculations of the distance between the walls. "A forward roll," he explained, "ending in a triple double back flip, should provide sufficient momentum to spring off the wall behind me, launch into a somer-saulting dive, and deliver a mighty blow to the door hinges, thus rendering them broken."

He took a deep breath and spread his arms. With a grunt of effort, he leapt high into the air and dropped down in a painful tangle of limbs on the floor. "Ow," said Timothy.

"Oh, Timothy," wailed Mum.

EPISODE SEVEN

WuuAAAAAA! WuuAAAAAA!

The alarm was sounding all around the building. In Laburnum Groves's dressing-room, Julie instantly put two and two together and came up with Matthew and Lloyd in deep trouble.

"Typical," she muttered to herself.

Ms Groves was lying on a pile of cushions, which were in turn lying on a large comfy sofa. One arm was draped over her eyes, while the other wafted in Julie's direction.

"Tell them to switch off that atrocious noise," she whined. "I presume the kitchen smoke detector has finally had a sniff at the charred nonsense that passes for an apple turnover in these studios." She pulled a couple of cushions over her head. "And hurry! Snoozle will be completely unnerved if this goes on any longer! Of course, I'm unnerved already.

The things I have to put up with –" And so on, and so on.

Snoozle was fully occupied chewing the frighteningly expensive carpet into a dribbly mess. Julie, thinking quickly, already had a plan worked out. While Ms Groves tried to block out the sound of the alarm with another couple of cushions and a headache pill, Julie hurried to the make-up table. She dabbed, powdered and pencilled to match Ms Groves's most glamorous look. She strapped on Ms Groves's platform shoes, grabbed Ms Groves's wig, then had a quick sort through Ms Groves's wardrobe and wriggled into a long, sparkly dress.

"Just going to give them a piece of your mind, Ms Groves," she called.

"Mhuh," grunted Ms Groves.

Slamming the dressing-room door behind her, Julie pranced across the studio floor. She'd seen every scene that Laburnum Groves had ever played, and now she'd get to play one for herself. Luckily, the dress hid the way her feet were slightly too small for the platform shoes.

Even with the alarm sounding in the background, she could tell that everyone had shut up. Laburnum Groves wouldn't have checked to see if they were all watching her, so neither did she. Arthur, the director, came bustling up to her, nervously picking at his woolly jumper.

"Labby, sweetie, it's lovely to see you, have you had a nice lie down, have you decided that I was right after all, darling?"

"No, I certainly did *not* have a nice lie down and no, I certainly have *not* decided that you were right after all," squeaked Julie, doing the voice very well indeed. "Did you bring my limousine round to the main entrance, as I demanded?"

"Er, well, yes, Labby, love," stammered Arthur, shuffling the pages of his script. "But, darling heart, we haven't shot a single frame. We can't keep filming your stunt double. The audience will get suspicious."

"Pooh to the audience," squealed Julie. "Are they rich and famous like me? No, they're bloomin' well not!"

"Oh, pleeeeease," squirmed Arthur. He stopped squirming long enough to examine her closely, smiling sweetly. "You know, Labby, I don't think I've told you how absolutely smashing you're looking today."

"Get me my limo!" cried Julie nervously. "I'm returning to my hotel, where I shall have a hot bath and shout at the manager!"

Arthur gave up, and buried his face in his hands. "Oh, very well. Off you go," he sobbed.

Julie stood there for a moment, sparkling. "Er, you'll have to escort me. I've, um, forgotten the way to the main entrance. There, you see! *That's* how angry I am with you! I've lost all sense of direction! The things you ghastly people put me through!"

Fighting back the tears, Arthur led her away. She did the walk pretty well, too.

"What a complete cow," muttered one of the camera operators under her breath.

At that moment –

– the alarm was switched off. It didn't make things any easier for Lloyd. He was still surrounded by a swarm of security guards, each of them heavily armed with the ability to give a really nasty Chinese burn. They towered above him, the peaks of their caps pulled low over their eyes. They managed to stare aggressively at him, all the same.

At the sound of footsteps behind them, they suddenly parted into two groups, to allow Mr Spite through. Even though the lighting was back to normal, shadows seemed to follow him down the corridor. The shadows were followed by Podmore. Mr Spite walked slowly over to Lloyd and did the most terrifying bit of looming Lloyd had even seen.

"Where are the others?" he said quietly.

Lloyd was too busy keeping his lower lip still to answer.

"Reopen this room," said Mr Spite to one of the guards. The guard stepped forward, entered a code into the panel by the door, and it slid open with a sharp hiss.

Matthew tumbled out into the corridor. Behind him, half the equipment was in flames. The other half looked like it would be in flames any second. Matthew staggered to his feet, coughing, his clothes smoking slightly and his face smeared with grime.

"Oh, deary me," he said. "We've ruined hundreds of thousands of pounds worth of gear. Sorry about that."

"Only an inconvenience, I promise you," smiled Mr Spite horribly. "All the programs, data and finished recordings were downloaded to my personal vault deep underground before the room was ... cleaned up. All part of our fail-safe system. The experiment is protected, this room no longer exists as evidence and you two are my prisoners."

"Well, we're simply quaking in our boots, aren't we?" cried Matthew. Lloyd wanted to tell him to belt up, but he couldn't get his mouth to work. Mr Spite moved close to Matthew, and glared at him.

"I don't like the tone of your voice, young man," he said quietly.

Matthew glared back. His voice was equally calm and low. "I wish that was all I didn't like about you," he said.

"You think you can defeat me?" growled Mr Spite. "Me? With the power to alter minds at my command?"

"What, you mean, today Void TV, tomorrow the world?" said Matthew.

"No," said Mr Spite. "I don't want the world. What would I do with it? There are so many places I would never want to go. The tops of mountains, the bottoms of oceans, Burger Shed. No, I don't want the world. Only its money. My mental rearrangement process helped me get control of this company and now it will help me get control of enough cash to fill an oil tanker. The Wheetie Puffs people paid me a fortune for last night's advert and after tonight's round of *Big Bob's Big Bonanza Quiz*, the Captain Zappo people will pay me another fortune. And beyond that is a long line of other people, with other rubbish to sell, begging for my services."

"I see, so you're basically just a thief," said Matthew.

Mr Spite seized Matthew tightly by the collar. His eyes narrowed, and his thin mouth twisted like a worm on a fisherman's hook. It was the same expression he'd used many years before, when he'd told his grandmother how he'd sold her dog to buy himself extra birthday presents.

"I could have you dropped down a well," he hissed slowly. "I could have your house burnt down. I could have your friends dumped in the sea in a wooden crate. It's all within my power."

"I'm not afraid of you," said Matthew quietly. Lloyd was amazed. Matthew really meant it.

"I know who you are," said Mr Spite, "and I know where you come from." He pointed a bony finger at Matthew. "You are Matthew Bland. And you," he added, his finger swinging slowly in mid-air, "are Martin Lloyd."

Lloyd was still too busy keeping his lower lip still to answer.

"So where in my building," snarled Mr Spite in a low whisper, "is Julie Custard?"

Julie was marching through Reception. Arthur the director scurried along beside her.

"Your limousine is outside, Labby, dearest," he said. "Have a lovely evening, and a peaceful sleep, and we'll see you in the morning, yes?"

"I'll think about it," cried Julie.

"Oh, Ms Groves," piped up the receptionist. "Ms Groves!" He waved a little wave at her. His smile bounced off his cheeks and nearly shot up his nose.

Julie turned (or rather swivelled, since she still wasn't used to wearing such enormous platform shoes) and held out a hand to him, just as Laburnum Groves had done to the lawyer in the tense courtroom finale of *Broken Justice*.

"Oh, Ms Groves," gushed the receptionist.

"I'm a huge fan!"

"What, not a receptionist?" said Julie, raising an eyebrow.

The receptionist laughed far louder and far longer than he needed to. At last he regained his composure and said, "Oh, Ms Groves, would you do me the gigantic honour of giving me your autograph?"

He delicately offered her a pen between thumb and forefinger. She took it and scratched a curly "With love, Labby Groves" in black ink across his teeth.

"Oh, Ms Groves, I'll never brush them again," he gasped.

"How revolting," she said brightly and swept out of the building, pausing only to free her sparkly dress from the revolving door.

"We've no idea where Julie Custard is," said Matthew casually. "At home washing her hair, or something."

Mr Spite turned to Podmore. "Seal the whole building off. Get guards to do a full sweep of every studio, every dressing-room, every blasted toilet! I want her found. And then…"

"Sir?" said Podmore, adjusting his glasses.

"And then, Podmore, I'd like you to arrange for these two … resourceful boys to receive a free gift."

"Free gift, sir?"

"Yes. A free visit to the insect farm at my home. The scorpions and cockroaches do so love having visitors. What a shame that visitors so rarely appreciate all those ... bites and stings. Arrange it, Podmore."

"Y–yes sir."

Guards grabbed Matthew and Lloyd by the arms and legs, and hoisted them up to shoulder height. Mr Spite quickly reached into Matthew's pocket, and pulled out a computer disc. He dangled it in front of Matthew's face for a moment, then tucked it away inside his jacket.

"You can't out-think me, Matthew," he smiled. He turned to Podmore. "Take them away."

As Julie sauntered out of the main entrance, she let out a silent "wow" whistle as she caught sight of the limousine. It was long, it was pearly white, and it was shinier than Mr Prunely's hair when he hadn't washed it for a few days.

The driver spotted her approaching, jumped out and held open the rear door for her. He raised his cap.

"Good afternoon, Ms Groves."

She almost toppled off her platforms as she bent to climb inside. The interior had large, soft, furry seats, with thick carpet covering the floor. Several gently curved panels were set into the polished wood that separated the front seats from the back. The driver clunked the door shut behind her and resumed his place behind the steering wheel. The air inside was cool. Not a single sound filtered through from the world outside. Julie lounged, exactly as Laburnum Groves had done as the wicked Lady Doonasty in *The Wicked Lady Doonasty*.

"Back to your hotel, Ms Groves?" the driver inquired politely.

"No. Drive round and round the building. Very quickly."

Julie prepared herself to answer a long string of polite inquiries …

"Yes, Ms Groves."

… but found she didn't need to. The limo glided into motion. The driver flipped the indicators and the vehicle gently turned at the corner of the building and accelerated along past the side entrance.

"Any particular speed, Ms Groves?"

"Um, just use your discretion, Mr Driver."

"Dennis, Ms Groves."

"Oh yes. Dennis. Forgot for a moment."

She shuffled over to the window and pressed her nose against it. She looked left and right, watching for signs of Matthew and Lloyd.

Matthew and Lloyd were watching for signs of Julie.

"She'll have thought of something brilliant," whispered Matthew, "and be on her way to rescue us."

"What if she's not?" quivered Lloyd. "What if she's been got, too? What if we all end up being fed to the scorpions?"

"If this was a really old war movie, I'd sock you on the jaw and tell you to pull yourself together, you dashed fool."

Lloyd wished somebody would pull him together. The guards were tugging at his legs so hard, and gripping his arms so tightly, he was sure he'd never walk or operate his games console ever again. Meanwhile, Matthew was trying to formulate an escape plan, just in case, by some weird error of fate, Julie WASN'T at that very moment knocking out guards and causing large explosions.

"Lloyd," he whispered. "Your mad scene from *Homework Overload*, please."

"What, now?" hissed Lloyd, eyes wide.

"Now," said Matthew.

Suddenly, Lloyd started twitching and thrashing, foaming at the mouth and uttering hideous cries of torment.

The guards ground to a halt and looked at each other, confused.

"Whassup wivvim?" said one.

"We're so scary, 'eez gone barmy," said another.

"Oh nooooooo!" screamed Matthew. "It's

happening again! He's got advanced Nail-shott's Syndrome! Caught it from an unripe sausage in the school canteen! It only flares up at times of extreme stress! Like now!"

"Hasn't 'ee got a pill or summat?" said a third guard.

"Pill, man, pill?" cried Matthew. "It's incurable! In thirty seconds he'll have grown teeth that'll make a man-eating shark look like a really sensitive vegetarian! He could bite chunks the size of Coventry out of any one of us! Run! Run for your lives!"

The guards looked at each other again.

"Are you having us on, Bland?" said a fourth.

"Are you going to wait around to find out?" cried Matthew.

"This run for your lives business sounds good to me," said a fifth, from the back.

Lloyd wriggled in a particularly mad way. He shook his head and dribbles of spit sprayed over the guards. As one, they yelled and ran for their lives.

Matthew and Lloyd had descended a nearby flight of stairs and dodged behind a rack of costumes before they even looked back. Matthew flopped to the floor, exhausted. He made a mental note to get more exercise, definitely, absolutely, this time for sure.

"Liked the spit," he gasped. "Nice touch."

"Thanks," said Lloyd. "I think I recognize

this bit. This is near where we came in!"

Meanwhile, the security guards had consulted Fearsome Frank's big medical book (kept for emergencies). They had discovered that Nailshott's Syndrome was a made-up disease, only ever contracted by prisoners making a getaway. A few minutes later, they realized they'd been tricked.

"Will you be requiring to return to the hotel at all today, Ms Groves?" inquired Dennis, after coughing a polite little cough to gain attention. Julie's face was still squashed against the window.

"Just keep on driving," she said. Her words fogged up the glass in front of her eyes. She rubbed it clear hurriedly. "No! Stop!" she called.

"Yes, Ms Groves."

The limo glided to a halt. Julie pressed a sensor on the armrest of her seat and the window slid down silently. Matthew and Lloyd had shot out of the building's side entrance, running as if a murderous mob were after them.

Julie leant out of the window and let out an ear-shattering whistle. At first, Matthew and Lloyd thought they were being attacked with some terrifying sound-wave device and dropped to the ground. Then they spotted the limo and hurled themselves into it through the window. They bounced upright off the seats.

"Quick! That murderous mob are right behind us!" wheezed Matthew.

"Move!" yelled Julie. Dennis put his foot on the accelerator and the limo gathered speed rapidly.

"Hi, Jules," said Lloyd.

"Who?" said Julie loudly. "I'm Laburnum Groves, and this is Dennis."

"Hallo, Laburnum, hallo, Dennis," said Matthew, spotting what was going on.

From behind them came the sounds of screeching tyres and revving engines. Everyone turned and looked out of the rear window. Lloyd covered his ears. A black van, packed with guards, was speeding across the car park after them. Huge red and yellow flames were painted along its sides. One of the guards had quickly chalked "VTV Revenge Squad" across the bonnet.

The van was joined by a car: a sleek, red sports model, driven by Podmore. It was the gadget-packed car they'd been using in Studio 3 to film the hugely popular spy series *Our Man From MI7*. Lloyd took one look and covered his eyes too.

Behind the spy car came a whopping great tank, a leftover from a World War II drama that had been finished off in Studio 1 the week before. A guard's head, wearing goggles and a helmet, poked out of a hatch at the top. Lloyd peeked out between his fingers, caught sight of it and clamped his arms over his head.

"Perhaps it might be wise to stop here, Ms Groves?"

They turned back and looked up ahead. Huge metal gates were closing, blocking the way out onto the road. "No!" shouted Julie. "Ram them!"

The gates were almost shut. With a crash of twisting metal, the limo slammed into them. The gates burst outwards, flying across the road. One spun off over a wall, the other crunched to a stop in the side of a lorry and was carried away to Rotterdam on the overnight ferry.

The limo turned sharply to move off into the traffic. Cars honked and swerved out of its way. They did a lot more honking and swerving when the flame-patterned van, the stunt car and the tank all roared into the road too.

"I'm starting to wish we'd just let them feed us to the scorpions," groaned Matthew.

EPISODE EIGHT

"...OK, thanks, Dave, and top story on the Radio Groove hot news chart this afternoon is, hey wow, a dramatic chase through town! Completely reliable eye-witness accounts from our reporters on the street say that a really posh car is being pursued by twelve camels, the Japanese Army and a giant man-eating dinosaur with teeth and everything! Cool! The police say they're taking no action, because they're in the middle of an important darts match down at the station. Hey, too bad. Back to you, Dave..."

"You know, this really is a lovely car," said Matthew, feeling the polished surfaces and soft seats inside the limo.

"Yeah, pity we've stolen it," mumbled Lloyd, shivering as fear ruffled up his hair and ran an icy finger down his neck once more.

The limo swung in a wide arc, overtaking a line of cars waiting at a red light. It was hurtling through the town centre now, surrounded by shoppers, traffic and buildings. Not a sensible place to go hurtling, on the whole. It whipped and weaved across a crossroads, barely missing an enormous lorry.

The spy car pulled up level with the van. Inside, Podmore kept one hand on the steering wheel while he flipped through the pages of an instruction manual with the other. He was trying to work out how to operate the rocket launchers hidden behind the headlights.

In the limo, Matthew was pressing buttons. One of the wooden panels behind the driver's seat flipped open to reveal a miniature fridge packed with food.

"Oooh, snacks," he cried.

"Matt, this is no time to eat!" wailed Lloyd.

"I missed my lunch!" protested Matthew, filling his face with a chicken and mushroom vol au vent.

"I'll be seeing mine all over again if we keep swerving about like this," groaned Lloyd. He glanced out of the window, saw the screaming faces of pedestrians flying past, and decided not to glance out of it ever again.

"Which direction do you require, Ms Groves?" asked Dennis.

Julie hesitated.

"Right!" she cried, decisively. The limo

swerved. It bumped over the pavement, gave two old ladies a terrible fright, and shot back out onto the road. The van, the car and the tank were hot on its bumper.

FFFwweeeeee-OOOOOOOSSHHH! KA-BLAMM!

Podmore had found the rocket launchers. A smoking black tube now jutted out where one of the car's headlights had been. The missile had made a crater, which the limo bounced violently in and out of. The missile had also turned a fishmonger's shop into a heap of bricks and bits of fish at the side of the road, which the limo narrowly avoided.

FFFwweeeeee-OOOOOOOSSHHH! KA-BLAMM!

The second blast knocked the limo sideways. The door next to Lloyd buckled inwards. Part of the roof ripped into flapping strips of metal and plastic. Dennis apologized for the bumpy ride.

"Why can't they leave us alone?" yelled Lloyd. "I'm not going to say anything! We've got no evidence any more!"

"Says who?" said Matthew.

"Says me!" wailed Lloyd. "That bloke who looked like a snake took the disc."

"He took the blank disc I put in my pocket as a decoy," said Matthew. "He didn't take the one in my left sock, did he?"

"You know sometimes, Matt, you almost

are a genius," smiled Julie. She felt quite proud of him.

Lloyd, on the other hand, felt sick. The sudden CLANG! that came from the back of the limo made him feel even sicker. They peeped over the seats.

A large metal claw, attached to the spy car by a thick cable, had been fired from under the car's bonnet. It had hit the boot of the limo and locked onto it. The cable tightened, pulling the two vehicles closer and closer together. The van was level with the back end of the limo. Its painted flames knocked against the buckled door beside Lloyd.

"Crumbs," said Matthew.

"They're not going to give up, are they?" said Julie.

"It's not fair," sobbed Lloyd. "I've got a Maths test tomorrow and I'm being chased by a killer TV executive!"

Podmore was becoming quite confident with the car's controls. He'd worked out how to fire the rockets, and he'd activated the Claw-O-Matic system ("keeps you in touch with suspects" the instruction book had said). Now he was sure he'd found the switch which would fire an oil slick under the limo, thus causing it to slip and loose speed.

He was wrong. It was the ejector seat.

Matthew, Lloyd and Julie lost sight of him when he, the driving seat and the giant coiled spring that was underneath the driving seat, catapulted to 12,000 feet. It was then that Podmore realized he'd made a second silly mistake.

"Can't see a parachute or anything," said Matthew, shading his eyes to get a better look.

"That's a silly mistake, forgetting your parachute," said Julie.

Luckily for Podmore, a jet plane was climbing to 12,000 feet in the airspace above the town. It caught the underseat spring neatly on its tail as it shot past. Unluckily for Podmore, the plane was from a flying school and spent the next six hours doing loop-the-loops, rolls and emergency dives.

Meanwhile, back on the ground, the limo was still attached to the spy car by the claw and cable. The van swerved out across the road. It began to overtake.

The tank shifted into top gear and gained speed, its caterpillar tracks whizzing. It hit the back of the spy car, which crumpled and flattened under the immense weight.

The cable jerked violently and the limo jerked with it. Dennis battled with the steering wheel, but was losing control. As the tank lurched closer, the claw suddenly ripped free. The limo bounded forward. The last shreds of the spy car disappeared in a mangled mess beneath the tank.

Meanwhile, the van had raced ahead. With

its tyres screeching, it swung around to block the limo's path.

"We're approaching the shopping centre, Ms Groves," said Dennis. "Is there anything you need to get?"

"There's so much stuff I need to get at the shopping centre!" cried Mum. "It'll be closed by the time we get out of here!"

Mum and Timothy were still held captive in their tiny wooden prison.

"There, there, Mother," said Timothy, straightening his shoe laces. "Never fear, for I have formulated yet another escape plan, based on various elements of my two weeks' work experience in engineering."

"Oh, Timothy," said Mum lovingly, "at least I have one son who can stay calm in a crisis and come up with another mother-saving idea."

Timothy burst into tears.

"I'm fibbing!" he blubbed. "I haven't the foggiest how to get us out of here! We're trapped! Doomed! Lost for ever!"

"Oh, Timothy," said Mum. "Pull yourself together!"

Timothy couldn't manage to pull himself together, so instead he went to pieces some more. Mum stuck her fingers in her ears to try to block out the noise. She started examining their prison in more detail.

"Timothy," she said at last. "You did check that this door is actually locked, didn't you?"

"Of course I did, Mother!" blubbed Timothy, dabbing his eyes with a hanky. "I'm not stupid, you know! Of course I checked! How could anyone be so utterly stupid as not to check! Mother, really!"

Mum turned the handle. The door swung open. They could now see a long and very battered limousine charging towards them.

The workmen's hut they'd been imprisoned in was hit by the limo at a speed that ought to have got Dennis arrested. Mum and Timothy had leapt onto the limo's windscreen and started screaming before the first fragments of hut had fallen to the ground.

They were in the middle of a building site, next to the shopping centre. The limo bumped jerkily over bags of cement, spinning and dodging to avoid the van and the tank. The tank, ideally suited to this sort of terrain, roared in a straight line across the path of the limo, bashing off its front bumper and smashing its lights.

"Hallo, Mum," said Matthew cheerily, with a wave.

"AAAAARRRRRRrrrrrrrgGGGGHHHH-HHHH!" said Mum, clinging to the windscreen wipers. Timothy said much the same, only slightly louder.

The limo skidded back onto the road and

went full-throttle for the entrance to the shopping centre. The entrance was exactly 1.25 millimetres too narrow for it. The paint along each side was neatly scraped away as it sped through.

"Very accurate driving, Dennis," said Julie.

"Thank you, Ms Groves."

The van flashed through the entrance at high speed, losing wing mirrors and side door handles on the way. The tank simply smacked into it and ground to a halt under the thirty-six tonnes of rubble that dropped on top of it.

The limo came to a sudden stop too, because the shopping centre was packed with people and Dennis had nowhere left to manoeuvre. The van came to a sudden stop because it ran into the back of the limo.

Mum and Timothy, still screaming (and taking the windscreen wipers with them), were flung off the limo as soon as Dennis stamped on the brakes. They shot into Millstone's book shop, through a display of large, heavy DIY manuals, and into unconsciousness. This saved Matthew the embarrassment of being told off by his Mum in public.

Two teenagers, nibbling on Burger Shed Cheese 'n' Chicken Specials, watched it all happening with mouths open, dripping ketchup down their T-shirts.

"Hey, I heard about this on Radio Groove," said one.

"Yeah, so did I," said the other. "So where's the dinosaur?"

"Could be that dude there, man," said one again. "Looks like a snake."

Mr Spite stepped out of the back of the van, ignoring any shoppers who happened to be fleeing in terror from flying mothers, smashed-up limos and nasty-looking security guards.

Matthew, Lloyd and Julie, meanwhile, dived out of one of the limo's broken windows, thanked Dennis very much indeed for all his help, and ran.

"I'll order a replacement vehicle for you, Ms Groves," said Dennis, bowing politely. "And an ambulance for me, if you'd be so kind as to permit it."

The security guards, headed by Fearsome Frank, were peering under tables at the Café Nosh, and rummaging through racks of umbrellas at Just for Rain. Mr Spite tapped Frank on the shoulder and pointed a bony finger at three figures hurrying away through the crowd.

"Oi, lads!" shouted Frank. "This way! Get 'em!"

"That was Fearsome Frank," gasped Matthew as the three of them took cover behind a small child.

"Did he say 'get 'em'?" said Lloyd shakily.

"Of course he said 'get 'em'," said Julie. "What did you expect him to say, 'let 'em run free as nature intended'?"

The small child's mum was starting to make a fuss, so they made a dash for Getting Shirty, the shopping centre's trendiest clothes shop. They pretended to be interested in buying ridiculously expensive sportswear.

The guards spread out through the crowd. Two of them marched straight into the clothes shop. They kept their eyes peeled as they crept past the trousers. They were on full alert as they sneaked between the jumpers and the underwear. They stopped, side by side, behind three youngsters who were shaking with fright, and who were keeping their faces hidden inside football shirts.

"Well, well, well, Harry, do you see what I see?" said a voice at Matthew's left shoulder.

"I do see what you see, Barry, I do," said a voice at Matthew's right shoulder.

"There's ten per cent off this ridiculously expensive sportswear," said Harry.

"Yeah. Says 'now only very expensive'," said Barry.

While Harry and Barry were choosing shorts to go with their peaked caps, Matthew, Lloyd and Julie crawled across the floor and out of the shop. They got to their feet once they were safely tucked away in the middle of a large, leafy bush outside World of Plants.

"We'll be safe tucked away here for a while," said Matthew.

Fearsome Frank reared up out of a terra-cotta pot, bellowing angrily, arms outstretched. Our heroes let out unheroic yelps, leapt out of the bush and rolled across the floor. Then they rolled smack into a dozen pairs of boots.

"I hope we're in a shoe shop," mumbled Matthew.

They weren't. They'd been got.

The guards hauled them to their feet, and surrounded them. Harry and Barry arrived, and surrounded them some more. They were in a forest of heavies, their noses unable to avoid the twin horrors of bad breath and cheap aftershave. A clearing appeared, into which stepped Mr Spite.

"Hallo, Matthew," he said, his lips uncurling into a grin like a baby lizard emerging from its egg. "How lovely to see you."

EPISODE NINE

"Hey, everyone! Look! It's Laburnum Groves!"

Matthew's yell echoed off the glass roof of the shopping centre. It hummed around the bargain rack outside House of Hats. It was heard by everyone between Sparkout Bedding Co. and Ron Sockett's Electrical Discount Warehouse. Matthew just had time to poke his tongue out at Mr Spite before crowds of shoppers descended on them.

Julie wasn't sure who she was angrier with: Matthew, for putting her in an awkward situation, or that bloke in the blue shirt over there, for ripping part of her sleeve and running away shouting "I got a bit of her dress! I got a bit of her dress!" Lloyd decided to cast himself in the role of Ms Groves's Personal Manager. He summoned up every ounce of acting talent he could muster in order to push people aside and yell at them very loudly in the face. His glasses almost fell off several times, so he put them in his pocket.

The crowd squealed and jostled. Heads popped up, trying to see over other heads. Lloyd, not having his glasses on, pushed and yelled in completely the wrong direction. Pens and bits of paper were waved wildly in front of Julie's nose.

"Will you sign this receipt from House of Hats, Ms Groves? It's for my blind sister!"

"I've seen all your films! I've seen all your films!"

"Is it true you're in the next *Batman* movie?"

By the time Mr Spite and the guards had managed to break free of the crowd, and Fearsome Frank had dragged Harry and Barry away from the queue for autographs, Matthew had very nearly achieved his objective: he was very nearly out of sight.

"There!" growled Mr Spite, catching sight of him as he disappeared around a corner.

"We'll get 'im, sir," said Frank, saluting. "We'll just pop back to the van and pick up some nasty pointed sticks to jab at 'im, sir, and then we'll 'ave 'im!"

"No," said Mr Spite. "You get your clumsy gorillas out of here. I'll deal with this."

He followed Matthew.

* * *

Matthew was sure he was being followed.

M. Bland in nail-biting suspense movie! Creepy music begins! Our hero looks furtively over shoulder! Deep shadows blot out places where bad guys might be hiding!

However, he wasn't in a nail-biting suspense movie. The only music was the tinkly stuff played around the escalators. The only furtive looks came from shoppers wondering what this pudgy kid was up to. Worse still, he doubted he could have laid his hands on a deep shadow even if they'd opened a branch of Deep Shadows R Us right next to him and had a half-price sale.

M. Bland in complete washout! "Am still on the run!" confesses terrified schoolboy. "And I still haven't had lunch!"

Movies weren't like this. Especially *his* movies.

He didn't know what to do.

So he went to the cinema. The Empire ("Your Multi-Screen Movie Emporium") adjoined the shopping centre and it was possible to reach it from the ground floor. Its name stood in tall, brightly lit letters above billboards marked COMING SOON and PENSIONERS HALF PRICE (MON A.M. ONLY).

As he hurried in, the noises of the crowds and the tinkly music in the shopping centre were suddenly stifled. His shoes made no sound on the thick carpet. All he could hear was his own rapid breathing and the distant rattle of gunfire coming from Screen 1. Movie posters covered the walls and a giant, glass-covered case in the centre of the foyer groaned under the weight of 7,512 bags of popcorn. It would have groaned louder if it had realized how much the 961 bars of chocolate weighed.

"Can I help you?"

The lady behind the ticket desk didn't bother to smile, and neither did her baseball cap. Across the cap was printed WELCOME TO THE EMPIRE! Her enormous hair stuck out at peculiar angles beneath it.

"Can I help you?" she repeated, miserably.

"Er, I'm not sure," said Matthew.

The ticket lady sighed. "Screen 1, *Death Squad Do Miami*. That's an 18, you can't see that one. Screen 2, *Mission: Unlikely*. That's a 15… Are you fifteen?"

"No."

"You can't see that one. Screen 3, *Pickles the Pixie's Toyland Adventure*. That's a U. You can see that one."

"I don't want to see that one," said Matthew.

"Screen 4, *Dinosaurs Eating People in Realistic Detail*. That's a PG."

"Sold!"

"It's full up."

At that moment, Matthew's suspicions about being followed were confirmed. He

113

spotted Mr Spite walking across the foyer. Mr Spite's view of Matthew was obscured by a pile of 2,512 mini ice-cream tubs. Matthew leapt behind the desk and crouched down behind the ticket lady's seat. Mr Spite sped past the ice-cream and closed in.

"Don't give me away!" whispered Matthew, urgently. "Please, I beg you. This is life or death. I mean it. If you want to help expose a terrible evil, if you want to see justice and truth prevail, please, please, please, don't give me away!"

"He's down here!" called the ticket lady.

Matthew jumped up and ran in a smooth, swift movement that would have earned a round of applause from the school athletics team. Mr Spite's snatching fingers brushed at his collar as he pounded along the long, silent corridor that led to Screen 2.

The sign on the heavy door at the corridor's end said, STAFF ONLY. CUSTOMERS ARE FORBIDDEN BEYOND THIS POINT. THIS MEANS YOU MATEY! Matthew hurled himself through, and slammed it back in Mr Spite's face.

This gained him half a second but lost him his nerves. The hissing roar of anger that followed him up the stairs to the Projection Room almost made him slip over.

The Projection Room was wide and brightly lit, with a low ceiling and polished floor. Four huge projection machines were loaded with giant, round spools of film. Each spool was set horizontally, and was roughly the width of a film-star-sized limo. Beams of shifting, multi-coloured light shone from each machine through glass panels in the walls, two to the left, two to the right. The machines hummed and rattled quietly to themselves, as if they were dead chuffed with the whole idea of being in the movie business. Everything was automated. The projectionist who was sup-posed to be looking after everything was off having a cup of tea with the cleaning lady, and was hearing all about the dreadful pains she'd been getting in her legs.

Matthew looked around frantically. There was absolutely nowhere to hide.

It was too late anyway.

With a snarl, Mr Spite's talon-like hands grabbed Matthew's neck. Matthew wriggled, but he couldn't free himself. Mr Spite's grip was too tight to be forced open. His out-stretched arms were too long for Matthew to be able to deliver a kick to the shins.

Guessing that a thin bloke like Mr Spite wouldn't be able to hold up someone of a slightly fuller figure for long, Matthew simply lifted his feet off the ground. Mr Spite, aided by the odd grunt, managed to keep him in mid-air for a few seconds, then the two of them tumbled forwards.

They were bowled heels over head. As

Matthew staggered to his feet, Mr Spite twisted over and reared up like a cobra ready to strike. His eyes were a blazing red.

"You really ought to watch your blood pressure, you know," said Matthew. "Stress is a killer."

"Where is it?" spat Mr Spite. "Where's the disc?"

"Realized I sold you a dud, huh?"

"I'll give you one chance, boy," hissed Mr Spite, pulling himself up to his full height. He loomed menacingly, with more loom than a knitwear factory and enough menace to get him straight through to the finals of the World Menace Championships. "Tell me where you've hidden that disc and I'll arrange for you not to be buried up to your neck in an ants' nest."

"I must say, you're ever so good at this looming menace business, aren't you?"

"WHERE IS IT?" Mr Spite grabbed Matthew by the scruff of the neck. With a sudden uncoiling of his arms, he hurled him against one of the projection machines. Matthew bounced off and hit the floor painfully. He wasn't sure whether the hollow clanging noise echoing in his ears came from the machine or him. Before he could decide, Mr Spite had dragged him to his feet and flung him against another machine. This time there was a crunching sound, as the whole thing rocked and shuddered.

Out in the auditorium of Screen 1, the audience suddenly felt sick as the picture in front of them rocked and shuddered. An old lady in Row C dropped her ice-cream.

Behind her in Row D were Mr Nailshott, Head of Modern Languages, and his girlfriend, Suzi. She was wearing orange lipstick and a skirt that could have been mistaken for a handkerchief.

"Ooo err, is that rocking supposed to happen?" said Suzi.

"Oh yes, my little sweetie pie," said Mr Nailshott. "I read about it in the reviews. The earthquake scene. Now come here for a cuddly wuddly."

Matthew dodged as Mr Spite's fist slammed into the wall, cracking the plaster. He slid across the polished floor, but lost his balance and slipped over into a heap beside the Screen 3 machine. Mr Spite was upon him in a second.

"Where is it, Matthew? Hmmm? Where is it?" he rattled. His pointed nose and serpentine eyes were millimetres from Matthew's face. "You know I mean what I say. I'll destroy you! I'll destroy everything! Why won't you TELL ME!"

Matthew simply stared back at him. His

expression was firm.

Mr Spite tightened his grip. "I will not have my carefully worked-out and technically perfect plans interfered with by a TALENTLESS NOBODY LIKE YOU!"

Matthew's eyes almost popped out of his head. This was partly due to the pressure of Mr Spite's hands on his throat, but mostly due to his utter and total disgust at being called a ... a...

"How dare you!" he yelled.

New-found strength seemed to flood through him. In moments, the two of them were on their feet, grappling. Matthew pulled Mr Spite one way, Mr Spite pulled Matthew the other.

They cannoned into the Screen 1 machine. It groaned, as if it was beginning to change its mind about the movie business. It swung sideways. Their struggles pushed it left and right across the floor until its beam was pointed at the opposite wall, shining a dazzling, out-of-focus kaleidoscope of light right across them.

Mr Spite had Matthew's chin gripped in the crook of his arm. Matthew could hardly move, hardly breathe.

"I'll kill you before I let you win," hissed Mr Spite. "Do you hear me, I'll KILL YOU!"

Out in the auditorium of Screen 1, the audience suddenly felt confused as the picture was replaced by the shifting silhouettes of two people fighting. The old lady in Row C dropped her hot dog. The soundtrack was still playing, pumping out gunfire and explosions.

"Which one's the good bloke again?" said Suzi.

"This is the worst fight sequence I've ever seen," said Mr Nailshott. "Look at those special effects, you can tell that's not real."

Matthew could feel the disc shaking loose from his sock. If it dropped out, if it clattered to the floor, if Mr Spite spotted it...

He tried to think of a brilliant idea. All he could think of was his sock.

What would the heroes in his movies do? They'd escape through a clever loophole in the plot, that's what they'd do!

And there was the loophole, right in front of him: "Spool Release".

The controls along the side of the Screen 1 machine were almost within his reach. He wriggled as much as he could, which wasn't much at all, really. Mr Spite's fingernails tore at his hair. He lunged, stretching out, willing his arm to grow. The tip of his middle finger swatted at the controls. And...

He flipped the Spool Release switch. With a sudden jerk, the giant, round spool of film on the Screen 1 machine unhooked itself and started throwing out hundreds of metres of action adventure in a spiralling, uncurling ribbon. Film fluttered and slid in all directions. Mr Spite, his head tied up in ten minutes of car chase, dropped Matthew and staggered backwards.

Matthew tried to untangle himself from the end titles, but only managed to get himself wrapped in the trailers for next week's screenings. Mr Spite thrashed wildly, but couldn't escape. Matthew pulled the disc from his sock and held onto it.

Out in the auditorium of Screen 1, the audience felt even more confused. The peculiar squiggling that had suddenly filled the screen for a couple of minutes was replaced by the shape of a young man, apparently covered in spaghetti, holding up his hands in triumph and yelling "Yeeeeaaaaahoooo! I win! I win!" The old lady in Row C missed it, because she was trying to retrieve her hot dog from under Row B.

"Is that the good bloke, then?" said Suzi.

"That's the worst acting I've ever had to sit through," said Mr Nailshott. "Yeeeeaaaaa-hoooo indeed. Now come here for a kissy wissy."

EPISODE TEN

The following evening, Matthew, Lloyd, Julie, Lloyd's parents, Julie's parents and Julie's baby sister were all gathered in the living-room at Matthew's house. Mum stepped over legs and around cushions, offering everyone cheesy nibbles and bite-size sausages on sticks. She'd covered up the bandages around her head with a yellow spotted scarf. She'd almost forgiven Matthew for the day before. But not quite.

"Matthew Bland! Sit there and don't speak."

Timothy, his head also bandaged, was up in his room sulking and writing miserable poetry. He'd been stripped of his school prefect's badge for being a big weed in the face of danger, and had decided not to come out of hiding until everyone went back to thinking he was great. So there's no chance of him appearing again before we get to the end of the book.

"Shh!" said Julie. "It's starting!"

(Presenter appears on TV screen. Looks very serious and speaks very seriously, wearing very serious suit.)

Presenter: Tonight on News Made Serious, *chickens and high voltage electricity. Can they be friends? Also, the second of our special reports on the world's ecological crisis, with Big Bob the Bouncing Clown. But first, the scandal surrounding Void TV. This major TV company, a rival of the channel you're watching now, is in a right load of trouble. The studios have been shut down and the head of the company is tonight in police custody. The entire world's media has been stirred into a frenzy by a shocking story, now brought to you with the help of Matthew Bland, the schoolboy who, along with two friends, blew the whole thing wide open. Over to our reporter, Claire Bluesea.*

(Cut to: outside the main entrance of Void TV. Police stand guard. One of them is trying to free his helmet from the revolving door. Reporter interviews M. Bland. M. Bland with hair combed neatly by Mum.)

Reporter: Matthew Bland, you're a keen *amateur film-maker. It was while lawfully going about your film-making business that you stumbled upon a secret that was, quite literally, mind-blowing.*

M. Bland: Yes.

Reporter: And you and two of your friends braved hideous peril, overcame incredible odds and triumphed against the forces of evil so that truth and justice would prevail.

M. Bland: Yes.

(Cut to: movie studio. L. Groves lounges in comfy chair. Snoozle wee-wees quietly in her lap.)

Reporter: Laburnum Groves, you're a film star. You were spotted making a getaway from Void TV. You've been accused of being in league with those responsible for the sinister plot uncovered by Matthew Bland and his associates. You've been billed for thirteen million pounds' worth of damage caused by your chauffeur-driven limousine.

L. Groves: It's all nonsense! I was in my dressing-room, recovering from a simply vile headache. That's a headache – not a tickle, not slight discomfort, but sheer, blinding agony! This ridiculous accusation has lost me a part in the next Batman *movie!*

(Cut back to: news studio. M. Bland pictured with TV screen, computer, editing gear etc. Holds disc packed with evidence.)

Reporter: You gathered evidence of evil doings at the highest level of Void TV. Tell us exactly what happened from the beginning, and demonstrate your findings with the help of this top-of-the-range equipment.

M. Bland: This particular story…

… we already know about. By the time the programme had finished, all the cheesy nibbles had gone and Mum had completely forgiven Matthew.

"I knew it," she said, dabbing her eyes with a paper napkin. "I always said my darling Matthew was the one to watch. 'You'll be a leading Hollywood director before you know it,' I always said, and I was right."

"Yes, Mum," sighed Matthew, gulping down the last of the bite-size sausages.

At school the next day, Matthew, Lloyd and Julie got the feeling they were being watched. They also got the feeling they were being talked about. Kids grinned at them for no apparent reason. The dinner ladies gave them extra mashed potato (which everyone except the dinner ladies thought of as a punishment). It was when teachers started to smile and wave that they became seriously worried. They met up on the bench outside the Science block after lunch to reassure each other that they weren't going barmy.

"Perhaps this is what it's like being famous?" said Julie.

"I thought we already were famous," said

Lloyd.

"Actually, I think we were *in*famous," said Matthew, thoughtfully.

Mr Prunely spotted them on his way to an urgent appointment with the Headmaster. He smiled and waved at them, and plodded over to the bench, picking dried-up bits of egg off his jacket.

"Hallo, Matthew, Julie, Martin. Saw you all on the goggle box last night. Terrific work! Really smashing!"

"Oh, that means so much to us, sir, thank you," said Matthew with a cheery grin.

"Jolly well done," said Mr Prunely. "Mind you, it all sounded quite alarming. I had to have a sit-down and a piece of cake after I'd watched the programme, I can tell you. I say, Mr Bland, it's all rather like the plot of one of your films!"

"If you say so, sir," said Matthew. "Good thing it wasn't like the plot of *Franken-Teacher*, then."

Mr Prunely laughed, but not too much. He still had terrible memories of seeing *Franken-Teacher*, and the havoc it had played with his lower intestines afterwards. He made a complete hash of changing the subject, because he said, "So, are you planning your next cinematic spectacular?"

Matthew looked up at the sky for a moment. He breathed deeply and was about to reply, but then noticed Dawn Gardner of 9C approaching. His mouth shut at the same time as Lloyd's dropped open. Lloyd snatched his glasses off his face and stuffed them into his pocket.

Mr Prunely suddenly remembered about his urgent appointment. He said hasty goodbyes to them all, and ran off to see Mr Nailshott. This was the wrong urgent appointment, but at least he had remembered it.

"Hello, Martin," said Dawn. Then she paused. "You are Martin Lloyd, aren't you?"

Lloyd nodded soppily at the patch of wall behind Dawn's head.

"I can never tell when you're not wearing your glasses. You look like a different person without them."

"Thank goodness," said Lloyd, to the waste-paper bin next to the bike shed.

"No, I mean they suit you. They bring out your character."

"Yeah, I think so too," said Lloyd. They were now back on his face. "I'm thinking of getting a bigger pair."

"Why didn't you wear them on telly last night? I didn't even realize it was you until this morning. Everyone in 9C was talking about it. My friend said that now I had a good excuse to come over and talk to you. So here I am."

"You were … waiting for an excuse?" said Lloyd. He couldn't believe his ears, so he tugged them a bit, but they seemed to be working OK. "Would you like to see the spectacles catalogue I've got hidden in my locker?"

"OK," said Dawn. "It's a shame they got your name wrong last night. Fancy calling you Lloyd."

"Yeah," said Lloyd. "Silly billies."

They wandered off, and although they weren't actually arm in arm, they were both thinking about it.

Matthew was looking up at the sky again.

"Well?" said Julie.

"Well what?"

"What's your answer to Mr Prunely's question? Have you got your next script written? It normally only takes you a couple of hours."

Matthew breathed deeply again. Julie wondered if she ought to call a doctor.

"You know," said Matthew at last, "I haven't thought about winning a major award for days and days."

"But that's what keeps you going," said Julie. "That's your goal, your inspiration."

"Hmmm," said Matthew.

Julie quickly looked up the number of the hospital in her pocket Filofax.

"I've been thinking about that," said Matthew. "Now that we've more or less saved the whole of civilization as we know it, it all seems a bit dull, being eaten by giant insects and so forth. Don't you think?"

"But I was going to say you can credit me as Julie Custard from now on. It's distinctive."

"You can be credited as Julie Custard, but how would you feel about making more earth-shattering documentary exposés? I mean, we'd be a formidable team, what with my film-making skills, your acting talent and … Lloyd. What would you say to the idea of facing appalling dangers, risking life and limb and generally getting into trouble on a regular basis?"

"When do we start?" said Julie.